Something's in the basement.

"Did you hear that?" Zack gasped.

"You mean the thunder?" Willy asked. He was hoping that what he'd heard was just his imagination.

"No!" Zack was shaking in his pajamas. "That!" He pointed to the air vent near the bunk beds.

This time, Willy didn't say a word. He just stood frozen as the sound drifted up from the basement and crept into his room.

Woo . . . woo . . .

Willy's heart started pounding so hard, he could feel it down to his fingertips.

Woo . . . woo . . .

Downstairs in the basement the train whistle was blowing. And there was no mistaking the clickety-clack of the wheels as the *Tiny Town Express* rounded the tracks.

DEADTIME STORIES™

Terror in Tiny Town

Terror in Tiny Town

A. G. Cascone

Published by Troll Communications L.L.C.

Deadtime Stories is a trademark of Annette Cascone and Gina Cascone.

Printed in the United States of America.

10 9 8 7 6 5 4 3 2

For Peter and Shirley Cascone,
who always taught their children
to follow their dreams . . .
and always made that possible

CHAPTER 1

Hurley the Hobo sat on his bench under the lamppost in Tiny Town. His haunting green eyes watched the boys' every move as they laid little Suzie Sparkle across the train tracks.

"Nooooooo! Don't kill me!" Willy Tyler put on his best goofy girl voice. *"I'm Margaret's favorite doll!"*

"Shut up, Suzie, you little freak." Willy's best friend, Zack Miller, laughed as he gagged Suzie Sparkle with the sparkly ribbon from her hair. "You're gonna die!"

"Too bad we can't tie Margaret to the train tracks instead of this stupid doll," Willy said.

"Yeah!" Zack agreed.

Margaret was the seven-year-old, pain-in-the-you-know-what little beast that Willy's parents called his sister.

Willy and Zack hated Margaret. Especially after two whole days of being trapped inside the house with her. The rain had been coming down nonstop, leaving them with nowhere to go to escape Margaret for more than a couple of minutes at a time.

Willy was sure Margaret would be tromping down the basement steps any second looking for him and Zack. But this time they were ready for her. This time Margaret wasn't going to get a chance to torture them. Because they were going to torture her first.

Willy couldn't wait to hear Margaret's blood-curdling scream when she saw her doll getting creamed. He was sure it would be better than anything in the horror movie he and Zack had wanted to rent.

Only Willy and Zack hadn't been allowed to rent the movie they wanted, because Margaret had thrown a tizzy fit right in the middle of the video store. Margaret had wanted to rent the same dumb princess movie she always rented. Willy's mom said it was way too late to watch two movies, so they'd ended up leaving with Margaret's movie. Willy's mom would do anything to shut Margaret up.

So Willy and Zack had decided that if they couldn't *watch* some horror, they were going to *make* some—just to get even with Margaret.

Zack was playing around with Suzie Sparkle's position on the tracks. "Maybe we should put her lengthwise. That way, the train will smash right into her head."

"Good thinking," Willy agreed. "Besides, if we leave her

sideways, her legs might knock over some of the pieces in Tiny Town."

Tiny Town was Willy's pride and joy. It was the biggest, coolest electric train setup ever. Willy's dad had even built a special table for it.

Tiny Town was actually a whole collection of towns that portrayed different times and places.

There were farm towns with cattle and cities with cars, old-fashioned streets and modern-day highways, Wild West ranches and old English castles, wide-open plains and mountains covered by forests.

The *Tiny Town Express* made its way through them all, crossing bridges and tunnels as it rounded the tracks.

"Watch out!" Willy hollered as Zack tried to lay Suzie Sparkle just the right way. "You almost knocked over Hurley!"

"Sorry, Hurley," Zack told the little hobo figure.

He glanced over at Willy. "So do you really like him?" He'd already asked this same question a million times.

"Are you kidding?" Willy said. "Hurley's a great present. He's the coolest guy in Tiny Town!"

Willy wasn't just saying that either. He had hundreds of tiny figures in Tiny Town, everything from knights in shining armor, to cowboys and Indians, to regular people in modern-day clothes. But Hurley the Hobo was definitely the best. He even came with a really cool reputation.

According to the little story card Willy found in the box, Hurley wasn't just a hobo. He was an outlaw who was wanted in every state of the Union for robbery, rioting, and wreaking havoc. There wasn't a town on the map that would have him, because wherever Hurley went, trouble was sure to follow.

Everything about Hurley was perfectly detailed, right down to the tiny bundle on the end of the stick that rested over his left shoulder.

But Willy thought the coolest thing about Hurley was his eyes. They weren't just painted on, like most of the other figures. They were made of glass. And they were so green, and so piercing, Willy couldn't help thinking they looked real. No matter which way Willy moved, Hurley's eyes seemed to follow him.

"My mother wanted me to buy you some dumb cowboy lady," Zack said. "But the minute I saw Hurley, I knew I had to get him."

"I can't believe your mom made you bring presents for everybody," Willy said.

"I told her it was stupid." Zack rolled his eyes. "But she told me you have to bring presents when you're staying at someone's house. It's the polite thing to do."

"Yeah, well, guess what," Willy said. "My mom's making me bring presents back to your house too. So you'd better decide what you want before she goes out and buys something really goofy."

"Too bad they didn't make us give each other presents *before* I moved away," Zack said. "Then we both would have gotten stuff every day!"

Willy and Zack had been best friends from the time

12

they started kindergarten. Zack used to live around the corner from Willy, but when Zack's dad got a new job, the family had to move to another state.

This summer Zack was staying at Willy's house for two weeks. Then Willy was going to spend two weeks at Zack's house. The best part was that Willy and Zack were going to ride the train back to Zack's—all by themselves.

"So what do you want?" Willy asked.

"I don't know." Zack shrugged. "You think you could talk your mom into getting me a ten-speed bike?"

Willy laughed.

"Shhh!" Zack said suddenly. "I think Margaret's coming."

"Tra, la, la, la laaaaaa!"

Willy cringed as Margaret's voice drifted through the vent in the basement. The vent system in Willy's house picked up every noise there was. Margaret's singing sounded like nails scratching a blackboard.

From what he could hear now, Willy figured Margaret was passing through the kitchen, headed for the basement.

"Quick!" he told Zack. "Get ready to flip the switch the minute she hits the first step."

A second later, the basement door flew open. Margaret started "tra-la-la-ing" her way down.

Zack pulled the switch. The train whistle blew as the *Tiny Town Express* began rounding the track.

Margaret's freckled face appeared over the stair railing. "You guys missed the best movie ever," she taunted.

Willy and Zack laughed.

"Oh, yeah?" Willy shot back. "Well, guess what. You're just in time for an even better show." In front of him, the *Tiny Town Express* started picking up steam.

Margaret narrowed her eyes. "What kind of show?" she demanded.

"A horror show," Zack answered. "Starring the one and only Suzie Sparkle."

"What are you talking about?" Margaret snarled as she reached the bottom step.

Neither boy bothered to answer. Instead they gave each other a high five as Margaret saw for herself.

The windows rattled as she let out the blood-curdling scream. "Moooooooom-myyyyyyyy!!!!" Margaret wailed. "They're killing Suzie Sparkle!!!!"

Zack had already anticipated Margaret's next move. As Margaret ran for the train to save her doll, Zack stepped right in front of her.

"Stay back, Margaret," he warned. He pointed his finger at her as he rubbed his feet furiously on the carpet. "Or I'll zap you good!"

Zapping was Zack's best talent. He was like a human ball of static electricity. And when Zack rubbed his feet on the carpet hard enough, his zaps hurt really bad.

Margaret stopped dead in her tracks. But she kept right on screaming. *Moooooom-myyyyy!* They're killing Suzie Sparkle! And Zack's trying to zap me again!"

"Forget about screaming for Mommy, Margaret." Willy laughed. "You better just call 911, because there's about to be a horrible accident in Tiny Town."

The three of them turned toward Tiny Town. The *Tiny Town Express* was rounding the last curve and heading down the track straight for Suzie Sparkle's head.

As the train sped past the tiny bench under the lamppost, Hurley the Hobo's haunting green eyes shifted again. Only this time they weren't following Willy. This time they were following the train.

CHAPTER 2

"What's going on down there?" Willy's mother yelled down the steps just as the *Tiny Town Express* crashed into Suzie Sparkle's head. The doll's sparkly face squished up like a pug dog's as her plastic skull caved in.

Margaret hit the stairs running. She was screaming and crying more than if she had been tied to the train tracks herself.

"Mommy!" Margaret shrieked. "Willy and Zack killed Suzie!"

Willy and Zack tried to keep straight faces while they denied Margaret's accusations. But Mrs. Tyler didn't want to hear about it. When Margaret went on a screaming, crying, ranting, raving tizzy rip, the solution was always the same.

"Bedtime for everyone!" Mrs. Tyler commanded.

Willy and Zack ran up the stairs. They'd already gotten even with Margaret, so they didn't really object to going to bed. Besides, there was an old monster movie coming on at eleven-thirty that they wanted to watch.

The two of them got ready for bed. Then Willy flicked on the TV.

It's the perfect night to watch a scary movie, Willy thought.

The teeming rain sounded like waves crashing down on the roof of the house. Lightning flashed through the darkness, and loud claps of thunder shook the walls around them.

"Check it out." Zack elbowed Willy. They were sitting on the floor leaning against Willy's bunk beds. "That giant tarantula guy is about to bite that kid's head off."

"Cool!" Willy laughed. He was dying to see what happened next.

But just as the giant tarantula guy opened his mouth, a huge bolt of lightning exploded outside. A second later the picture on the TV screen got all fuzzy.

"Aw, geez," Zack groaned. "We're missing the best part!"

Willy glanced at his window. "Didn't that lightning look close to the house?" he asked. "Maybe we should turn off the TV."

"Why?" Zack asked.

"Because lightning might come right through the TV and kill us," Willy said.

17

"No way." Zack laughed. "Who told you that?"

"I don't know," Willy answered. "Somebody did."

"Yeah, well, that somebody must have been a moron," Zack told him. "There's no way lightning can come through a TV and kill you."

Suddenly, Willy's entire room lit up as if the sun had hit the earth. Only it wasn't the sun. It was the worst lightning Willy had ever seen.

The TV made a loud pop as an enormous explosion of thunder echoed all around them. Then Willy's room went pitch black.

"Geez, oh, man!" Zack was so startled, he practically hit the ceiling. "That lightning almost came right through your window!"

"I told you we should have turned the TV off!" Willy cried.

"Well, we don't have to worry about turning it off now," Zack shot back. "Everything in the whole house is off!"

Willy jumped up and headed for the window to see if everybody else's power was out too.

But before Willy could look outside, a strange sound came from *inside* the house. And the sound coming from inside the house startled Willy even more than the next terrifying clap of thunder that suddenly exploded overhead and practically stopped his heart.

"Did you hear that?" Zack gasped.

"You mean the thunder?" Willy asked. He was hoping that what he'd heard inside the house *before* the thunder was just his imagination.

"No!" Zack was shaking in his pajamas. "That!" He pointed to the air vent near the bunk beds.

This time, Willy didn't say a word. He just stood frozen as the sound drifted up from the basement and crept into his room.

Woo . . . woo . . .

Willy's heart started pounding so hard, he could feel it down to his fingertips.

Woo . . . woo . . .

Downstairs in the basement the train whistle was blowing. And there was no mistaking the clickety-clack of the wheels as the *Tiny Town Express* rounded the tracks.

CHAPTER 3

"Somebody's down in the basement playing with the train set!" Zack whispered. He swallowed hard. "I sure hope it's your dad."

"There's no way my dad is playing with that train set, you moron!" Willy informed Zack. "You want to know why?" Willy walked over to the light switch and flicked it on and off. "That train set runs on electricity. And in case you haven't noticed, we don't have any!"

Woo . . . woo . . .

The boys glanced at each other as the train whistle blew again.

"*We* don't have any electricity," Zack said nervously. "But Tiny Town sure does."

"Maybe the power downstairs is hooked up to a different circuit," Willy suggested. He grabbed a flashlight from his desk drawer. "Come on," he told Zack. "Let's check it out."

Willy and Zack made their way down the hall past Willy's parents' room. Willy didn't need to shine his flashlight into the room to know that his parents were still asleep despite the bad thunder. He could hear his mom's even breathing and his dad's loud snores. If someone really was in the basement playing with the train, it wasn't his dad.

A picture of the giant tarantula guy flashed through Willy's mind. Maybe he should wake up his parents. Just in case. Only Willy wasn't about to tell Zack that the stupid monster movie was getting to him. Zack would laugh in his face.

They headed for the stairs.

Willy hit every light switch along the way. Nothing happened. The lights stayed out.

Now Willy was starting to get really nervous.

If Tiny Town *was* on a different circuit, it was on a different circuit from every other light switch in the whole house.

Is that possible? Willy asked himself.

"Maybe I was wrong!" Zack whispered suddenly. He grabbed Willy's arm to keep him from opening the basement door. "Maybe something really weird *is* going on down there!"

"Like what?" Willy said.

"I don't know," Zack answered. "Maybe that giant tarantula guy is down there or something!"

Willy couldn't believe it. Zack was just as freaked out

by the monster movie as he was!

"Yeah, right," Willy said, trying to act cool. "The giant tarantula guy is playing with the train set. Grow up, will ya."

"Fine," Zack snapped. "Don't believe me. But if he bites off our heads, I get to say I told you so!"

Willy took a deep breath as he opened the door slowly. He was trying hard not to think about what Zack had said.

He reached for the light switch. But the light didn't flick on.

Woo . . . woo . . .

The train whistle sounded in the pitch-black basement.

"I've got a real bad feeling about this," Zack said. He started to back away.

"We have to go down there," Willy insisted. "We have to find out what's going on!"

Willy started down the steps, with Zack inches behind him. Halfway down, Willy shined his flashlight in the direction of Tiny Town.

Willy gasped so suddenly, it made Zack scream.

The *Tiny Town Express* was whipping around the tracks faster than Willy had ever seen it move before. Creepier still were all the tiny little lights that seemed to be shining from every tiny little window in Tiny Town.

But there aren't any lights in Tiny Town! Willy thought. *Even when the electricity is working!*

Suddenly the *Tiny Town Express* screeched to a complete stop.

Then every tiny light in Tiny Town went out.

CHAPTER 4

Willy whirled to face Zack. "Did you see that?"

Zack's eyes were so wide, Willy thought they'd pop right out of his head.

"Something really weird *is* going on down here!" Willy went on. He didn't dare move a muscle. He just stood there, shining his flashlight at Tiny Town.

But now Tiny Town was totally dark. Totally quiet.

Willy started to take another step.

Zack reached out to stop him. "What are you doing?"

"I want to get a closer look," Willy told him.

"Yeah, well, you're not leaving me standing here all by myself!" Zack grabbed the back of Willy's pajamas.

They both headed cautiously down the stairs.

Willy kept swinging the flashlight around as they made their way toward Tiny Town. He wanted to make sure that nothing jumped out at them—like the giant tarantula guy.

But the basement was still. There was no sign of anyone, or any*thing,* lurking about.

Willy pulled open the storage closet next to Tiny Town's table. There was no one hiding in there either. Just lots of toys.

"I told you there was nobody down here," Willy said, relieved.

But Zack still looked spooked. "That means the *Tiny Town Express* started all by itself," he pointed out. "That's even creepier!"

Willy nodded. Zack was right. "Maybe it's plugged into a socket that didn't lose power until now," he suggested.

"Then how do you explain this?" Zack pointed to the metal power box sitting next to the train set.

Willy couldn't believe his eyes. The power switch that ran the train was turned to "off." The *Tiny Town Express* really had been running with no electricity at all!

"And what about all those tiny little lights in all those buildings?" Zack kept gnawing away at Willy's nerves. "How do you explain them? Huh?"

Willy shined the beam of his flashlight across Tiny Town. Maybe some of the buildings had lightbulbs inside that he didn't know about.

But Willy didn't see a single one.

He was about to check inside the train station when the tiny bench under the lamppost caught his eye.

Hurley the Hobo was gone!

CHAPTER 5

"Zack, look!" Willy gasped. "Somebody took Hurley!"

"What do you mean, somebody took Hurley?" Zack shoved Willy over so that he could see for himself. "This is too weird," he said. "Hurley's gone. But his little bundle is still there."

Willy nodded. The tiny hobo's bundle and stick were on the bench right where Hurley had been sitting.

Just then, the lights in the basement snapped on. Willy and Zack screamed as if the giant tarantula guy was coming to get them.

"Willy? Zack?" a voice called from the top of the stairs.

Willy was so shaken, it took him a second to realize it was his mother, not a monster.

"What are you boys doing down here so late?" Mrs. Tyler asked, heading down the stairs.

"Something really weird happened, Mom," Willy told her.

"Yes, I know," she said. "The storm knocked out the power for a little while."

"Not that," Zack told her. "Something *really* weird."

"Yeah," Willy broke in. "After all the power went out, the *Tiny Town Express* started to run!"

Willy's mother stood halfway down the stairs. She looked at Willy as if he were crazy. "That's impossible."

"I know," Willy agreed. "But we saw it with our own eyes!"

"Yeah, Mrs. Tyler," Zack jumped in. "I think this train set is haunted or something."

Willy's mom laughed. "I doubt that, Zack. Maybe the lightning caused some kind of power surge that made it go on."

Willy had to admit that sounded like a pretty logical explanation.

"But we saw lights in all the little buildings too," Zack pointed out. "And those buildings don't have any working lights. How do you explain that?"

"You probably just saw the reflection of Willy's flashlight," Mrs. Tyler answered. "Either that, or I shouldn't have let you two watch that giant tarantula movie."

Willy grinned. Now that his mom was here, the whole thing seemed pretty dumb. Her explanation about the lights made a whole lot of sense.

But Zack wasn't ready to give up yet. "What about Hurley?"

"Hurley?" Willy's mom asked. "Who's Hurley?"

"Hurley the Hobo," Willy told her. "The guy Zack brought for me."

"What about him?" she asked.

"He's gone!" Zack told her dramatically. "But his bundle is still here!"

"I bet Margaret took him," Willy told Zack.

"Come on, you two," Mrs. Tyler said. "It's almost two o'clock. You can check with Margaret about Hurley tomorrow." She turned and headed up the steps. "See you in the morning."

"Margaret is going to pay for this," Willy whispered to Zack as he headed up the stairs.

Zack looked around one more time, then hurried after Willy.

The next morning, Willy and Zack were ready for Margaret. But they weren't ready for Willy's mom.

"Good morning," Mrs. Tyler said as the two boys stepped into the kitchen.

But Willy could tell by the frost in her voice that there was nothing good about it at all.

Margaret sat at the kitchen table with a bowl of cereal in front of her and a mean little grin on her face.

"You two have a lot of explaining to do," Mrs. Tyler growled.

"For what?" Willy said. "What's going on?"

His mother glared at him.

"You know full well what I'm talking about," she

snapped. "Just look at this kitchen! It's a total disaster area! And I just cleaned this floor the other day," she went on. "Now it's all sticky and covered with crumbs. Not to mention that there's more food on this floor than in the cabinets! Why in the world would you do something like this?"

Willy took a good look around. Half-eaten cookies littered the tiles. So did seven apple cores, two banana peels, and three empty bags of corn chips. In fact, there was food—or the remains of food—everywhere. It looked like the cafeteria after the food fight on the last day of school.

"We didn't do this," Willy protested. "No way, Mom."

"Oh really?" she shot back. "Then how do you explain that?"

She pointed at the floor in front of the freezer. A carton of ice cream lay on its side. The lid was flipped open, and melted chocolate ice cream oozed all over the floor. Standing in the goo were about a dozen little people from Tiny Town.

"Your toys are everywhere," his mother told him.

Willy could see she was right. Not only were the little people standing in the goo, they were on the counter, on the table, and under the table. Every place where food was spilled, at least one little person from Tiny Town stood right in the middle of it.

"There was even one in my cereal," Margaret whined. "He fell out when I was pouring it into the bowl."

"Mom, I swear, Zack and I didn't do this," Willy said again.

"Then who else could have done it?" she snapped.

Willy and Zack answered at the same time. "Margaret!"

"Oh no!" Willy's mother hollered. "Don't you try to blame Margaret for this. She was asleep last night when you two were wandering around down here. And she was still asleep this morning when I got up. Margaret couldn't have done this."

"Well, we didn't do it either," Willy insisted.

"Then I suppose you expect me to believe that these little people walked up here all by themselves and made this mess," his mother said.

Willy didn't answer her. *Why bother?* he thought. *She's already decided that Zack and I are guilty.*

"Fine," his mother snapped. Her icy voice sent a chill up Willy's spine. "Collect your toys and get out of the kitchen so I can clean up this mess."

Willy shot a deadly look in Margaret's direction. Now she was really going to get it.

He didn't say a word as he and Zack picked up the residents of Tiny Town. But in his head he was already making plans for revenge.

Willy frowned when he saw the fat little mayor from Tiny Town Hall in the puddle of melted ice cream. His head was twisted to the side as if he were looking over his shoulder. And his short, pudgy legs were bent into a sitting position.

Willy couldn't imagine how Margaret had even done such a thing. The Tiny Town mayor was made out of plastic—plastic that wasn't supposed to bend!

As Willy reached for the mayor, he noticed something else. Something really strange.

There were tiny chocolate footprints everywhere.

It was as if the little people from Tiny Town really *had* been walking around by themselves!

Only that was impossible.

Or so Willy thought.

CHAPTER 6

"We can't let Margaret get away with this," Zack told Willy.

"No way," Willy agreed. "I just wonder where that little beast hid Hurley."

Willy and Zack had managed to put Tiny Town back in order, but Hurley the Hobo was still missing.

"She probably hid him up in her room," Zack said.

"Yeah, well, if Margaret doesn't give Hurley back," Willy replied, "she's never going to see Suzie Sparkle again."

"What are you going to do?" Zack asked.

"Watch," Willy told him.

Willy went over to the corner of the basement where his father kept his tools and got a small folding ladder. He carried it to the other side of the room and set it up.

"Give me Suzie Sparkle," he told Zack.

Zack grabbed Suzie Sparkle from the corner where they'd tossed her when they were cleaning up Tiny Town. He handed her over to Willy, who was standing on the ladder.

"Margaret will never find her up here." Willy laughed. Then he pushed up a ceiling panel and slid Suzie Sparkle in. He put the panel back in place carefully so no one would suspect it had been moved.

"Great hiding place," Zack said.

It was Willy's favorite. No one ever thought to look for stuff in the ceiling.

"What else can we do to Margaret?" Willy wanted even more revenge.

"What other toys does she like?" Zack asked.

"The Weevils!" Willy ran into Margaret's territory to get them.

"Weevils?" Zack laughed. "What are Weevils?"

"Stupid little dolls that live in this pocketbook house." Willy showed him a purple plastic purse.

"Are we going to hide them in the ceiling too?" Zack asked.

Willy thought about it for a minute. "Hey! What if we hide all of Margaret's toys up in the ceiling?"

"That would be pretty funny," Zack answered. "But Margaret's got a ton of toys. If we put them all up there, the ceiling might cave in."

"Good point," Willy said. "Besides, we ought to do something different with the Weevils. Something that would really drive Margaret nuts."

"You mean like running them over with the train?"

"Like that," Willy answered, his eyes lighting up. "But much, much better."

"What?" Zack asked eagerly.

"There's going to be a hanging in Tiny Town." Willy grinned. "The whole Weevil family is going to pay for Margaret's crimes."

The first thing they needed was a gallows. There was one in the Wild West part of Tiny Town, but it was too small for all the Weevils. Besides, Willy wanted to hang them right in the center of Tiny Town, in front of Town Hall. That way Margaret would see them as soon as she stepped downstairs.

"We can build a gallows out of Margaret's building logs," Zack suggested.

Willy liked that idea. Using Margaret's logs for the gallows to hang her doll family would really send her into a tizzy. They even took it one step further. The rope they would use to string up the Weevils would come right off Margaret's butterfly kite.

Willy and Zack hanged the whole Weevil family, even their little dog. And they assembled all the people of Tiny Town in Town Square to watch.

Just as they'd strung up the last Weevil, the basement door opened.

Willy and Zack exchanged glances. This was it—the moment they'd been waiting for!

But it was Willy's mother, not Margaret.

"Willy!" she called from the top of the stairs.

"Yeah, Mom," Willy answered, trying to sound normal. They were dead meat if she came down and caught them hanging the Weevils.

"I'm going to the food store," Mrs. Tyler said. "And I'm bringing Margaret with me. I expect the two of you to behave while I'm gone."

"Okay, Mom," Willy called back.

The basement door closed again.

Willy and Zack waited until it was completely quiet above.

"*Now* can we go upstairs and get something to eat?" Zack said. They'd been downstairs all morning and hadn't eaten a thing.

Willy reached the kitchen first.

The two boys didn't just get *something* to eat. They got *everything*. They went through the kitchen like locusts, grabbing peanut butter, jelly, bread, milk, cookies, potato chips, pretzels, and the last two bags of Margaret's gummi snacks. Then they brought it all back downstairs with them.

"So what do you want to do after we eat?" Zack asked as they got to the bottom of the stairs.

But Willy didn't answer. His attention was focused on Tiny Town.

"What the heck is going on down here?" Willy mumbled.

Zack noticed it too. "Hey! What happened to the Weevils?"

Willy couldn't answer. He just stood there, staring at the nooses dangling from the gallows.

The strings had been cut, and the Weevils were gone!

CHAPTER 7

"Somebody cut the Weevils down!" Willy gasped.

"Margaret!" Zack growled.

"How could Margaret have done this?" Willy demanded. "She's out food shopping with my mother, you moron!"

"Well, *somebody* did it," Zack said. "Just like *somebody* messed up the kitchen."

"Well, it wasn't Margaret, and it wasn't me or you." Willy's eyes darted around the basement, and a shiver went up his spine. He couldn't shake the feeling that he and Zack weren't alone.

"Do you think there's a burglar in the house?" Zack's voice dropped to a whisper.

"Burglars break into your house to steal things. Not to mess up the kitchen and play with your toys!" Willy replied.

"Then maybe your mom was right," Zack said. Willy heard panic creep into his friend's voice. "Maybe the little people are walking around here all by themselves! And maybe somebody in Tiny Town cut down the Weevils!"

Willy laughed, but inside he was panicking too. What if what Zack was saying were true? What if the little people really had left the footprints in the kitchen?

No way!

Willy wasn't about to believe something so ridiculous. "My mother wasn't serious when she said that," he told Zack.

"Yeah, well, I am," Zack said. "It's the only thing that makes any sense."

"It makes about as much sense as having our heads bitten off by a giant tarantula guy," Willy shot back.

"Then you come up with a better explanation," Zack challenged.

Willy racked his brains for one.

"You did it!" he accused Zack a minute later.

"How could I have done it, you idiot?" Zack said. "I was upstairs with you getting stuff to eat, remember?"

"Well, there's got to be some kind of logical explanation for this," Willy said. He stared down at Tiny Town, trying to figure out what it was.

Just then something caught his eye. A small piece of paper, about the size of a postage stamp, was stuck to the door of Town Hall.

Willy reached for it.

"What's that?" Zack asked, looking over Willy's shoulder.

"I don't know," Willy answered.

"It looks like a note!" Zack said. "Maybe the burglar left it!"

Willy rolled his eyes. "It does not look like a note."

"Does so," Zack insisted. He pulled the tiny paper out of Willy's hand and examined it. "I can see little letters."

"What does it say?" Willy asked.

"I don't know," Zack answered. "I can't read it. The writing's way too small. We need a magnifying glass."

Willy remembered there was one in the tool cabinet and hurried to get it. He held the magnifying glass over the tiny piece of paper.

Zack was right. It was a note, but it wasn't from a burglar.

"What does it say?" Zack prodded impatiently.

Willy could barely choke out the words.

"It says, 'Town Meeting tonight at midnight.'" Willy swallowed hard before he read the last line. "And it's signed, 'Hurley.'"

CHAPTER 8

"I swear I didn't write the note!" Zack insisted for the ten millionth time. "Look." He made an *X* across the front of his chest. "I cross my heart and hope to die. Okay? Does that make you happy?"

"No," Willy told him. "I still think you were trying to scare me."

It was getting close to midnight. The two of them had spent the whole day trying to figure out what was going on in Tiny Town. The only explanation that made any sense to Willy was that Zack had written the note.

Zack fell back onto the bed, exasperated. "I told you already, I couldn't have done it," Zack insisted. "I was with you the whole time!"

"Not when you went to the bathroom you weren't," Willy pointed out.

"Yeah, but I already proved to you I didn't do it," Zack told Willy. "There's no way I can write that small! I can't even write that neatly when I write big!"

Willy hesitated. Zack had a point there.

"I'm telling you," Zack insisted. "Hurley the Hobo wrote that note. Or there really is some kind of wacko burglar in the house who likes to play with your toys and mess up the kitchen."

Willy suddenly looked at the clock on his nightstand. It was ten minutes to twelve, almost time for the town meeting. "Come on," he said, grabbing his flashlight and heading for the door. "Let's go see who *really* wrote that note."

Zack stood up slowly and followed Willy.

By the time they got to the basement door, Zack was panicking. "I don't think we're invited to this meeting," he said nervously.

"I'll tell you what," Willy said. "We'll sneak down real quietly, so that nobody sees us, okay?" Then he turned off his flashlight. "We won't even turn the lights on."

Zack nodded, but he still looked unsure. "I guess so," he began. "But . . ."

Willy turned the doorknob before Zack could say anything more. The basement door creaked open. The noise made Zack gasp so loudly, Willy jumped nearly three feet.

"Stop being such an idiot," Willy whispered loudly. "It was only the door! Now shut up, or my parents will hear us!"

"Sorry," Zack whispered back.

Willy started down the steps, with Zack right behind him. Halfway down, Willy came to a complete stop.

The basement was pitch black and totally quiet. As Willy's eyes started to adjust to the dark, he could see Tiny Town.

It was just as dark and just as quiet as the rest of the basement. And totally still.

Willy looked at his watch. Thirty seconds until midnight. Willy held his breath as the seconds ticked by.

Then, at the stroke of midnight . . . nothing happened. Nothing at all. Midnight came and went without any sign of life in Tiny Town.

Willy and Zack waited.

And waited.

And waited.

Until Zack finally waited himself right to sleep on the stairs.

By two-thirty in the morning, Willy had had enough waiting too. He and Zack had been imagining things. Tiny Town was *not* alive.

Willy turned around and dragged Zack back up to bed.

Zack crawled up to the top bunk. Fifteen seconds later, he was snoring like a buzz saw.

Willy pulled the pillow over his head to get away from Zack's snoring, but it didn't help. Now he could hear Zack talking in his sleep, mumbling something about Tiny Town.

Willy kicked up at the top bunk to shut Zack up. "Wake up!"

But Zack let out a long, loud snort.

Willy kicked up again. This time it worked.

"What the heck are you kicking me for?" Zack growled.

"You're snoring like crazy. And you're dreaming about Tiny Town," Willy informed him. "You're talking in your sleep!"

"I am not talking," Zack insisted. "I'm sleeping!"

Just then, Willy heard another voice. And it definitely wasn't Zack's. This voice wasn't coming from the bunk bed above—it was coming from across the room.

It was coming from the air vent that led down to the basement!

CHAPTER 9

"Did you hear that?" Zack yelped, springing up like a shot.

Willy nodded, terrified.

"I told you I wasn't talking!" Zack said nervously.

"Yeah." Willy's voice trembled. "But somebody was!"

Willy and Zack didn't move. They just sat staring at the vent, their eyes wide open in horror.

Willy tried to tell himself he hadn't heard a voice. It was just his imagination. Or the air conditioner rumbling.

But Zack was convinced they'd heard something else.

"Someone was definitely talking," he said. "I told you those little people were alive!"

"Come on." Willy jumped out of bed. "We have to go down there."

"Are you out of your mind?"

"It's the only way to know for sure what's going on," Willy declared.

"I don't want to know for sure what's going on," Zack shot back. "And I definitely don't want to *see* it!"

But Zack didn't have a choice. Willy wasn't about to go back to the basement alone.

Willy and Zack tiptoed their way through the house a second time.

"Listen," Willy whispered as he and Zack pressed their ears against the basement door. "It's completely quiet. It must have been the air conditioner or something."

"Great," Zack muttered. "Then let's go back to bed."

Willy knew Zack was about to turn and run. He grabbed Zack's pajama top. "Oh, no, you don't! We're going down there!"

Willy pulled open the basement door. This time he made sure he turned on the light.

Willy and Zack took the steps one at a time. Below them the basement was as quiet as it had been at midnight. By the time they'd reached the bottom, Willy was feeling a lot better.

Until they saw Tiny Town.

"Tell me it was the air conditioner now!" Zack gasped.

Willy couldn't believe his eyes.

Every person from Tiny Town was crowded around Town Hall. The Weevils were there too, standing on the front steps with the strings from the gallows still wrapped around their necks.

Even more frightening was the sight of Suzie Sparkle.

She had gotten out of the ceiling and was standing in Tiny Town like a sparkly, smush-headed giant.

But the most terrifying sight of all was the one Willy feared most, the one that proved beyond a shadow of a doubt who really had written the note.

Standing in front of the crowd was Hurley the Hobo. His haunting green eyes glared up at Willy.

CHAPTER 10

"Tiny Town is alive!" Willy shouted at his parents.

But it was no use. They didn't believe him. Even after he and Zack had told them everything that had happened.

"What are you trying to tell me?" Willy's mom chuckled as she started clearing away the breakfast dishes. "That your tiny toys really are walking around this house by themselves?"

That was *exactly* what Willy had been trying to say, even though it sounded crazy to him too.

"You two are such weenies." Margaret laughed at them.

There was nothing worse than being laughed at by a bratty little sister. It took all of Willy's self-control to stop himself from reaching over and slugging Margaret.

"You know what I think?" Mr. Tyler said as he got up and put on his jacket to head off to work. "I think you guys have been cooped up inside way too long." He shook his head in amusement. "Your imaginations are working overtime."

"I think your father's right," Willy's mom agreed. "You guys are starting to go stir-crazy. Today's finally a beautiful, sunny day. Why don't you get dressed and go outside for some nice, fresh air."

It wasn't a suggestion. It was an order. Whenever Willy's mother said, "Go outside for some nice, fresh air," what she really meant was, "I can't stand to have you in this house for one more minute."

Mrs. Tyler wouldn't even let the boys go down into the basement to check on Tiny Town. As soon as they were dressed, she herded them right out the back door into the yard.

"I don't want to see you inside until I call you in for lunch," she told them. "Understood?"

"What are we supposed to do out here?" Willy moaned.

"Why don't you go for a bike ride," his mother suggested as she slid the glass door shut.

"I don't want to go for a bike ride," Willy huffed as he plunked himself down in a lawn chair.

"What *do* you want to do?" Zack asked, sitting in the chair next to Willy's.

"I don't know." Willy shrugged.

For a few minutes it felt like the old days, when Zack lived around the corner and the two of them spent most of the summer complaining about how there was nothing to do.

Willy picked up the Frisbee lying near his feet and started twirling it on the tip of his finger.

"Throw it here," Zack called as he got up and headed across the lawn.

Willy tossed the Frisbee to Zack. It went sailing right over Zack's head.

Willy laughed as Zack stumbled and fell on his butt trying to jump for it.

"Very funny," Zack grumbled, getting to his feet and brushing himself off. "Where did it land?"

"Over there." Willy pointed toward his mother's vegetable garden. "Be careful not to step on any of the plants," he told Zack. "My mother will kill us."

Zack stood at the edge of the garden and reached in to grab the Frisbee.

Suddenly he let out a scream. "Willy!"

Willy glanced over. Zack's eyes were fixed on the ground. There was a horrified expression on his face.

"You'd better come over here and look at this!" Zack yelped.

Willy started toward the garden. He figured there was a dead bird or a mole on the ground. The cats in the neighborhood were always catching and killing small animals.

"You're not going to believe this," Zack whispered as Willy came up beside him.

Zack was right. Willy couldn't believe what he was seeing.

It wasn't something dead. It was something much, much worse.

CHAPTER 11

Scattered among the bean stalks and rows of lettuce were dozens of Tiny Town pioneers. Nearby were miniature log cabins and corrals full of animals.

Willy looked at Zack. Zack looked at Willy.

Not only were the little people from Tiny Town moving around *inside* the house, they were moving *out* of it too! The pioneer people from the Wild West were taking over the vegetable garden!

At the moment the figures weren't moving, but Willy was sure that they had been.

A horse-drawn wagon loaded with strawberries was parked next to the strawberry patch. Standing behind it was a little man about to load another strawberry onto the wagon. Other men and women stood inside the patch, posed as if they'd been picking strawberries too.

"Your mom's got to believe us now," Zack said.

"No." Willy shook his head hopelessly. "She won't."

"She will if we show her," Zack protested.

"Show her what?" Willy asked. "What is there for her to see?" He answered his own question. "Just a bunch of toys all over her garden. She'll think we put them here."

"But we didn't," Zack protested. "There's got to be some way to convince your parents that the little people from Tiny Town are alive."

Willy sighed. "My parents will never believe it unless they see it with their own eyes," he told Zack.

"Yeah, but *we* haven't even seen it," Zack pointed out. "The Tiny Town guys never move when we're around."

"I guess they freeze when we show up," Willy said.

Zack looked around at the little people. "Do you think they're watching us right now? And listening to every word we say?"

Willy didn't want to know the answer.

He squatted and looked at the little man behind the wagon. It was just a plastic figure, a toy, Willy reminded himself.

"Touch him," Zack said. "See what happens."

Willy reached out slowly, half expecting the little man to attack his hand. But nothing happened.

Willy knocked the strawberry out of the man's hands. The little man fell over, but he didn't move.

Willy picked him up. "See?" he said to Zack. "He's plastic."

Willy tried to move the little man's arms and legs. But they wouldn't budge.

49

Zack picked up one of the other figures and did the same thing, with exactly the same results.

"I don't get it," Zack said.

"Neither do I," Willy told him. "But I think we ought to bring these guys back to Tiny Town and see if anything else is going on."

"We're not allowed in the house. Remember what your mom said?" Zack reminded him.

"So?" Willy blew it off. "Tell my mom that you have to go to the bathroom. Then sneak down into the basement and unlock the outside door for me. If we're real quiet, my mom will never know we're down there."

Zack ran off to put the plan into action, still holding the little man he'd picked up.

Willy started collecting the rest of the figures. He took as many as he could carry to the back door of the basement. Zack wasn't there yet, so Willy went back to the garden to get another load.

It took four trips to get all the people, animals, houses, and wagons. Still there was no sign of Zack.

Willy was about to go after Zack when he finally heard someone on the other side of the door turning the bolt. A second later Zack's head appeared.

"What took you so long?" Willy said.

"I really did have to go to the bathroom," Zack told him.

"Did you check out Tiny Town?" Willy asked.

"No way!" Zack answered.

"Come on." Willy picked up some of the stuff he'd

brought to the door. "Let's put these guys back where they belong."

"Let's just hope everything else in Tiny Town is the way it's supposed to be," Zack said.

But as Willy headed across the basement, he had a feeling that was too much to hope for.

He was right.

CHAPTER 12

"Uh-oh," Zack gasped as he stood staring down at the castle in Tiny Town. "Something tells me these little pioneers moved outside for a reason!"

Willy's jaw dropped.

The castle was sitting in the middle of the Wild West, where the pioneers used to be. The little knights were standing in front of the castle with their swords drawn. It was as if they were guarding their territory.

"The knights must have kicked out the pioneers!" Willy said.

"I bet they did," Zack agreed. "There's no way those pioneer guys could fight the knights."

"Why not?" Willy asked. "It's not like the knights are bigger."

"What are you, a moron or something?" Zack said.

"The knights are wearing armor. Plus, they've got swords."

Zack had a point. The knights really could kick the pioneers' butts if they wanted to.

"I bet they had a war down here last night, after their little town meeting," Zack went on.

"Then how come the knights didn't just slaughter these pioneer guys?" Willy asked.

"Who knows?" Zack shrugged. "Maybe the pioneers ran away first."

"Maybe," Willy said. "Only how come everything else is moved around too?"

"Beats me," Zack answered. "Maybe everybody in Tiny Town was fighting over territory."

Willy couldn't believe that he and Zack were even having this conversation. Tiny toys didn't walk and talk and write little notes calling town meetings! And they didn't have wars either!

"This is crazy," Willy said. "How can this be happening?"

Zack didn't have an answer for that one.

Neither did Willy.

"Yeah, well, Tiny Town isn't staying like this," Willy said. "That's for sure."

Willy picked up the castle, keeping his eye on the knights. He wanted to see if any of them would make a move to stop him.

They didn't. They just stood there, looking as stiff as the plastic they were made of.

"What are you doing?" Zack asked.

"I'm putting the castle back where it belongs," Willy told him. "There's no way I'm going to let these stupid little toys ruin Tiny Town."

"What if they don't want things back the way they were?" Zack asked.

Willy rolled his eyes.

"I'm serious," Zack said. "What if they get mad and try to get even with you?"

"Cut me a break." Willy laughed. "They're toys! Besides, if we put everything back the way it was, we can see if they move stuff around again."

Willy plunked the castle down in the countryside where it belonged. Then he reached back over to the Wild West to grab a handful of knights.

"You might be able to kick the pioneers' little butts," Willy told the knights in his hand. "But you definitely can't kick mine." Willy placed the knights next to the castle.

Zack laughed as he grabbed his own handful of knights. "Yeah, you little weenies," he told them. "You do what we say or we'll kick *all* your little butts!"

Willy nodded. He and Zack were a good four and a half feet taller than any of the tiny figures in Tiny Town. If the little people came alive again, Willy and Zack could definitely show them who was really in charge.

Willy reached for one of the plastic dragons that had been perched on top of the castle. "Okay, pal," he said. "Party's over. You're going back where you belong."

But as Willy wrapped his fingers around the dragon's little body, he felt it squiggle!

Before he could react, two razor-sharp teeth cut right through his skin.

The dragon was alive! And it was biting into Willy's finger so deep, it was drawing blood.

CHAPTER 13

"*Y*eoooooooow-ch!"

Willy jerked his hand so hard and so fast, the dragon went flying across the room.

"That dragon just bit me!" Willy screamed at Zack.

"What do you mean, that dragon just bit you?" Zack dropped the dragon he was holding.

"He bit me!" Willy repeated.

"Let me see," Zack said.

Willy held out his finger. The wound didn't look anywhere near as bad as it felt. There was only one little drop of blood and two tiny bite marks.

"You sure you didn't just stick yourself or something?" Zack asked.

"I'm telling you," Willy snapped. "That stupid thing bit me!"

Willy glanced over to where he'd flung the dragon. It was lying on the floor next to the table.

Willy leaned over slowly, expecting the thing to leap up at him. But the dragon just lay there, looking completely harmless, completely lifeless.

Zack studied the dragon from a safe distance. "Maybe we should just leave them *all* alone," he suggested nervously.

"No," Willy said firmly. "We can't tiptoe around these stupid little toys. Besides, Tiny Town is mine, not theirs."

With all the courage he could muster, Willy reached down and picked up the dragon. This time nothing happened. He put the dragon back on the castle and reached for a house that didn't belong where it was.

Willy was beginning to wonder if he and Zack were losing their minds. Or if the basement was haunted by some kind of psycho ghost who just liked to drive kids insane.

But no matter how freaked out Willy was, he was determined to show the little people who was boss.

"Grab those pioneers and put them back in the Wild West," he told Zack.

"Okay," Zack said. "But if one of them tries to bite me or something, I'm blaming you."

"Fine," Willy said. "Just do it." Then he reached out to grab some of the pioneers himself.

Only something stopped him.

Something bad.

Something that definitely did not belong in Tiny Town.

CHAPTER

14

"Zack!" Willy held his breath as he pointed to the biggest, fanciest house in Tiny Town. "Look!"

Zack was so startled, he dropped the pioneers to the floor. "What's the matter now?"

Willy didn't answer. He just pointed to the terrible sight.

The evil Weevils had moved all their stuff from their pocketbook house into the Tiny Town mansion. The whole place was redecorated. And nailed to the wall of the Weevil kids' bedroom was Mr. Tyler's prized possession—something no one was allowed to touch.

It was an original Babe Ruth baseball card, signed by the Babe himself. Willy's dad kept it in a frame on his desk. Only now, it was hanging in the Weevils' new house like a poster—by a tiny little nail that was driven through the tip of Babe's nose.

Zack's face turned a sickly pale. "Your dad's going to kill us for this!"

"He's going to do worse than kill us," Willy shot back. "My grandfather gave him that card when my dad was a little kid!"

"Maybe we can fix it up and put it back before he notices it's gone," Zack suggested.

It was the only thing they could do. Mr. Tyler would never believe the Weevils had done it.

"Let's just hope it's not ruined," Willy said.

Willy picked up the house and shook it. Hard.

The Weevils came crashing to the floor.

"I hate you little Weevil creeps!" Willy shouted as he kicked the entire family across the room. Then he reached into the house. He pried the tiny nail from the tip of Babe Ruth's nose as gently as he could.

"Got it," Willy sighed as he pulled the card from the house.

The nail mark was barely noticeable. Without looking closely, there was no way to tell there was a hole. It looked like a dust speck sitting on the tip of the Babe's nose.

Willy and Zack sneaked up the stairs and headed for the study. All they had to do was get the card back into its frame. Luckily, Willy's mom didn't hear them. She was up in her bedroom helping Margaret put together a costume for her stupid dance recital.

The second Willy and Zack reached the study, they headed for the desk.

The frame was nowhere to be seen.

Willy and Zack searched the room in a panic. Still no frame.

"Now what are we going to do?" Zack whispered.

Willy had no idea.

"Maybe we could buy a new frame," Zack suggested.

Willy shook his head. His father might not notice the Weevils' nail hole, but he'd definitely notice a new frame.

"Come on," Willy said. "Maybe the Weevils took the frame too. Maybe it's somewhere in Tiny Town and we just didn't see it before."

Willy and Zack headed back to the basement to search every inch of Tiny Town.

They discovered all kinds of things that didn't belong there. Weird things. Things like Margaret's fancy hair combs and Willy's mother's silver peppercorn mill. But they didn't find the frame.

"We're dead," Willy told Zack. "Without that frame, there's no way we can put this card back."

The basement door creaked opened.

Willy jumped.

"Are you guys down here?" Mrs. Tyler called from the top of the steps.

Willy shoved the card into his back pocket. He was terrified that his mother would come downstairs and see it.

"Yeah, Mom." Willy tried not to sound guilty.

"I thought I told you to play outside," she scolded them, but she didn't come down.

"We were," Willy answered. "We, uh, just came in to get the soccer ball."

"Well, it's almost lunchtime anyway," she said. "Why don't you come up and eat before you go back out."

"Okay, Mom," Willy called back.

"Now what?" Zack whispered.

"Let's go hide the card in my room. After lunch we can figure out what to do with it," Willy said.

Willy and Zack sneaked past the kitchen without being noticed. Then they tiptoed up the stairs and down the hall without making a sound.

Until they got to Willy's room.

Willy gasped loudly.

Sitting in the middle of Willy's dresser, right out in the open where everyone could see, was the frame they'd been searching for. And taped to the center of the frame was another little note from Hurley the Hobo.

Willy's heart sank to the pit of his stomach as he rushed to his desk to grab the magnifying glass. With all that was happening, he hadn't even thought about Hurley. And that was a big mistake. Because Hurley the Hobo was definitely thinking about him.

"What does it say?" Zack asked nervously.

Willy peered through the magnifying glass in horror.

The words were perfectly clear.

"'Leave Tiny Town alone!'" Willy's voice trembled as he read Hurley's note. "'Or you really *will* have a war on your hands!'"

CHAPTER 15

"Maybe we should call the police," Zack suggested.

"And tell them what?" Willy demanded. "That a toy hobo is threatening us?"

"Yes!" Zack answered. "Threatening people is against the law. And we've got the note to prove that Hurley's threatening us!"

"And what do you think the police are going to do when they finally stop laughing?" Willy asked. "Arrest Hurley?"

Zack's face turned red. "Well, maybe we ought to show the note to your mom before something really bad happens around here."

"My mom's not going to believe it either!" Willy said. "Nobody's going to believe that Hurley wrote this note. Not without proof anyway."

"So what are we going to do?" Zack asked.

It took Willy the rest of the afternoon to find an answer. But he did. And he found it in his dad's study while he and Zack were putting back the baseball card.

"My dad's camcorder!" Willy exclaimed. He couldn't believe that he hadn't thought of it sooner. It was the perfect way to get the proof they needed. The camera was sitting right on his dad's shelf.

"What about it?" Zack asked.

"The Tiny Town people don't move around when we're watching them, right?" Willy started to explain.

"Right." Zack nodded.

"So, what if we set up the camcorder to record everything that happens when we're *not* watching them?"

Zack smiled. "That's brilliant!"

"I know." Willy smiled back. "We'll have all the proof we need."

Willy and Zack decided to set up the camcorder to run overnight. That was when the little people seemed to do most of their moving. Besides, Willy wasn't supposed to play with the camcorder, so he and Zack had to wait until everyone was sound asleep before they could sneak it out of the study.

Setting up the camera was a piece of cake.

They put it on the shelf across from Tiny Town and pushed the record button.

Willy left the closet light on to make sure there'd be enough light in the room for the camera to catch everything that was happening.

Willy and Zack waited up for hours with their ears glued to the vent in Willy's room. Every creak made them jitter.

But there wasn't a voice to be heard. If the Tiny Town people were up to something, they were being awfully quiet about it.

Willy was exhausted. There was no way he was going to stay awake all night. Besides, he was sure that the camcorder was doing its job. If something was happening down in the basement, they'd see it in the morning.

Willy set the alarm clock for six. Then he and Zack climbed into their beds.

Willy didn't remember falling asleep. But it felt like only a minute had gone by when the alarm clock started blaring in his ear.

Willy and Zack hit the basement running. They didn't even bother checking Tiny Town to see if anything was different. They just grabbed the camcorder and headed for the VCR in the family room.

"Keep your fingers crossed," Willy told Zack as he pushed the play button.

The tape started to run. Tiny Town was lifeless.

"Fast forward a little bit," Zack told Willy.

Two seconds later they saw Tiny Town coming to life. Every window in every house lit up. So did every street-light. All around the castle, tiny torchlights started to burn. Little people poured out of every house and building, laughing and shouting as they gathered in groups.

The *Tiny Town Express* started up. It began to make its way around the tracks, through every village and town. This time it wasn't speeding. This time it was moving around the tracks slowly and deliberately. It stopped every few feet to pick up crowds of tiny passengers.

Willy could hardly believe his eyes. He sat there staring, too stunned to speak.

Zack didn't say a word either. He was as spooked as Willy.

It wasn't long before every person in Tiny Town had made his way to Town Hall. Some by train. Some in tiny little cars with tiny little headlights. The knights and the cowboys rode in on horseback. The miniature helicopters Willy had gotten for Christmas carried the little army platoons.

It looked like something really big was happening in Tiny Town.

"People of Tiny Town." A deep voice suddenly cut through the rumble of the crowd. "Listen to me."

Willy froze as Hurley the Hobo appeared from the doors of Town Hall.

"If you want to stay alive," Hurley's voice boomed, "you must do as I say!"

Willy and Zack exchanged worried looks.

"Why should we listen to you?" a tiny voice from the crowd shouted back.

"Because I've seen this kind of thing happen before, in lots of different towns," Hurley answered. "And unless you people start taking action now, you're always going to be pushed around by those horrible humans!"

"Listen to Hurley," another little voice piped up. "Those two ugly monsters tried to hang us the other day. It was Hurley who saved us."

"Uh-oh," Zack mumbled. "It's one of the evil Weevils! And he's talking about us."

Just then, a voice as irritating as Margaret's pierced Willy's eardrums.

"We really should listen to Hurley," it cried. "He's *sooooooo* cute!"

"Ew, gross," Willy said. "It's Suzie Sparkle!"

"Hurley may be cute," another woman's voice bellowed from the crowd, "but he's an outlaw. He's ruining Tiny Town by letting all kinds of riffraff move in. Like the Weevils. They don't belong here. Those horrible humans dumped them on us!"

"We're not the only ones who hate the Weevils," Willy muttered.

"We're going to need all the help we can get." Hurley spoke again. "And we're going to need as much strength as we can find. It's the only way to win!"

"What kind of strength does he think he'll find in Tiny Town?" Willy asked Zack.

Zack didn't have to answer. Because Hurley did.

"We're bringing in outside forces," Hurley informed the crowd. "Starting with the biggest, strongest, most frightening life forms we can find."

"What the heck is that supposed to mean?" Zack said.

"Move him in," Hurley shouted. Then he pointed above the crowd toward the other side of the room.

Willy watched as dozens of little men hoisted tiny ropes. Willy could see the men struggling and panting as they pulled. And pulled. And pulled.

But Willy couldn't see what the men were pulling up until they hoisted it all the way to the top of the table.

"What the heck is that?" Zack yelped.

Willy let out a breath as he saw what it was. "It's Margaret's Mookie Monster."

The boys watched the tiny men pull Margaret's Mookie Monster over to the train tracks. Giant sparks shot up from the tracks as the Mookie Monster crossed into Tiny Town.

"Look!" Zack cried. "The train tracks are shocking him to life!"

Willy watched in awe as the monster's googly eyes popped out of his head like a cartoon character. His tongue rolled out of his mouth, across the table, and down to the floor. Then he started gurgling as if he were blowing bubbles underwater.

A final shock sent the Mookie Monster rocketing straight up to the ceiling. Then he bounced off it like a giant, hairy Superball.

Ice-cold fear ran through Willy's veins.

Hurley the Hobo really was planning a war. And he was starting to bring to life an army of his own.

CHAPTER 16

The boys watched the rest of the tape, but they'd already learned what they needed to know. Tiny Town *was* alive. And the little people who lived there weren't very friendly.

"What are we going to do?" Zack asked as Willy snapped off the TV.

"We've got to get my parents," Willy answered. "They've got to see this."

Willy picked up the remote and rewound the tape so it would be ready to play the second his parents arrived in the room.

Then Willy charged upstairs to their bedroom, with Zack right behind him.

"Mom! Dad!" Willy knocked on the door. "You've got to wake up! You've got to come see this!"

"What is it?" his father asked.

"What's wrong?" his mother cried out at the same time.

"It's Tiny Town!" Willy answered them. "It *is* alive! It really is!"

"Not again," Mrs. Tyler groaned.

"It's too early for jokes, boys!" Mr. Tyler snapped.

Willy was much less worried about his father's anger than he was about what was going on in the basement. "This isn't a joke," he insisted, trying to make his parents believe him. "You've got to listen to us. Something really strange is going on in this house. And we've got proof."

"What kind of proof?" his father asked, still not sounding too happy.

"A video," Zack told him. "Wait until you see it. You're not going to believe it."

Willy's father opened the door. "I'd better believe it," he told the boys. "Or the two of you are going to be in big, big trouble."

Willy's mother got up too.

"Hurry," Willy told them.

But his parents didn't hurry. They moved incredibly slowly.

If only they had hurried, Willy's parents might have been able to see the videotape. But by the time they got downstairs, it was too late.

CHAPTER 17

"What is the meaning of this?" Willy's mother demanded, tapping her foot angrily on the floor.

Willy and Zack stared at the mess in front of them. The family room was practically buried in shredded videotape.

"You guys have gone too far this time," Mr. Tyler said sternly.

"We didn't do this," Willy said.

"Let me guess," Mrs. Tyler said coldly. "The little people from Tiny Town did it."

Willy looked around for something to prove to his mom that it was true. But there wasn't a single little person to be seen.

"They *must* have done it," Zack insisted. "They probably didn't want you to see the tape we made of them."

"You made a tape?" Mr. Tyler asked.

Willy and Zack nodded.

"How?" he wanted to know.

"We set up the video camera down in the basement before we went to bed," Willy admitted.

His father noticed the camera lying on top of the TV and headed across the room to get it.

"You're not supposed to touch that camera without permission," Mrs. Tyler reprimanded Willy.

"It's not a toy, Willy," his father added, picking up the camera to inspect it. "This is an expensive piece of equipment. I hope you didn't damage it."

"We didn't, Dad," Willy assured him. "We were very careful with it. I promise. All we wanted to do was see what goes on in Tiny Town while we're all asleep."

"Well, I can certainly see what goes on while *I'm* asleep," his mother said. "I'm surprised at you boys. And disappointed too. Your behavior these past few days has been horrible."

"I'm not so sure we should let you go to Zack's house, Willy," Mr. Tyler chimed in. "We certainly don't want Zack's parents to have to put up with this sort of nonsense."

"Dad, please," Willy begged. "You have to let me go to Zack's house. We've been planning this trip all year!"

"Well, let's see if your behavior improves," his father said.

"And you can start by cleaning up this mess," Mrs. Tyler added. "I expect this room to be immaculate by the time I come back downstairs." She started to leave the room, then abruptly she turned back. "I don't want to hear one more word about Tiny Town. I mean it." Then she really did leave, with Mr. Tyler right behind her.

"We're in big trouble now," Zack said.

"Yeah," Willy agreed. "And not just with my parents."

"Tell me about it," Zack said. "These little people mean serious business."

"How did they do this?" Willy asked. "How did they destroy the tape so fast?"

Zack shrugged and started scanning the room. "They've got to be around here somewhere."

The two of them didn't have to look long before they found the culprits. They were hiding behind the TV.

CHAPTER 18

Two little soldiers dressed in camouflage hung from a rope that ran up the back of the TV. The rope was secured to the top of the set with a small grappling hook made out of paper clips.

"They're the ones who destroyed the videotape," Willy exclaimed.

Zack nodded. "What's the deal with these little people?" he said. "They're getting totally out of control."

"We've got to find a way to stop them," Willy agreed.

"How can we do that?" Zack asked. "We don't even know what got them started in the first place."

"Yes, we do," Willy told him. "Thanks to the tape."

"That's right." Zack picked up on Willy's train of thought. "Margaret's monster came to life the minute he crossed the tracks into Tiny Town."

"It's like there's some kind of force field around Tiny Town," Willy said.

"But how did it happen?" Zack asked. "You've had Tiny Town forever, and nothing weird ever happened before."

"It started the night of the storm," Willy reminded him. "The lightning must have done something that made Tiny Town come alive when the rest of the power went dead."

"So why aren't the toys *always* alive then?" Zack asked. "They're alive only some of the time."

It was a good question.

"Maybe they're only alive at night," Willy suggested. But that couldn't be right, he realized. The pioneers had been out in the middle of the day. And it had been dawn when the two soldiers attacked. "Or maybe they can only go so far out of Tiny Town before they lose their power."

"That sounds more like it," Zack said. "And if that's what happens, then we've been stupid, because every time we find them outside Tiny Town, we put them right back in."

"Well, we're not going to do that anymore," Willy told him. "In fact, as soon as we clean up this mess, we're going downstairs to take Tiny Town apart."

"Good thinking," Zack said. "That'll take care of those little people once and for all."

"Yeah," Willy agreed. "If Hurley wants a war, he's got one. And we're going to win."

Willy and Zack cleaned up the family room as quickly as they could. They collected the shredded videotape and the empty cassette and tossed them into the garbage.

Then they got the soldiers and headed down to the basement. Only this time they didn't go down there like two frightened kids, nervous about what they might find. This time, they went down like an invading army to conquer the enemy.

As usual, Tiny Town was still.

"I guess we should take the track apart first," Willy told Zack.

Zack nodded his agreement and reached out to start. But the instant his fingers touched the track, there was a huge crackle of electricity.

Willy watched in horror as a giant spark sent Zack toppling backward onto the floor.

CHAPTER 19

"Zack!" Willy screamed. "Are you all right?"

"I think so," Zack said in a shaky voice. He sat up slowly. "But I got zapped pretty badly. There really must be a force field around Tiny Town. There's no way we're going to be able to get those train tracks apart."

"We have to," Willy said.

"Are you crazy?" Zack shrieked. "I almost got fried! There's no way I'm touching that thing again, and I don't think you should either."

"There's got to be some way to protect ourselves," Willy said. Then he thought of it. "Rubber gloves!"

"Huh?" Zack looked at Willy as if he were crazy.

"Rubber doesn't conduct electricity," Willy explained. "So maybe if we wear rubber gloves, we'll be able to touch the tracks without getting shocked."

"That sounds like a bad idea to me," Zack said, shaking his head.

But Willy was already off and running. His mother kept a pair of rubber gloves in the basement on the shelf above the washing machine.

He grabbed them and slid his hands into them as he headed back toward Tiny Town. He hoped his idea would work.

"Don't do it, Willy," Zack pleaded.

But Willy reached out for the track. His hand was shaking as he forced himself to touch a finger to the track. Willy braced for the shock of his life. But nothing happened.

He touched a second finger to the track. Then a third. Finally he closed his whole hand around it. The gloves worked!

Willy took the entire track apart in no time at all.

"Now what?" Zack asked.

"Now we pack up all this stuff in boxes," Willy told him. "And just to be safe, we'll tie all the boxes with string and lock them in the cabinet."

Luckily, there were lots of storage boxes in the basement. Willy's mother was a neat freak, who always insisted that things be put away properly. Usually that was a real pain, but for once it came in handy.

Zack wouldn't touch the tracks or the train. He started packing up people instead.

"I wish we didn't have to do this," Willy said suddenly.

"I know what you mean," Zack sympathized. "Tiny Town was the coolest."

"Until it came alive," Willy sighed.

"Yeah," Zack agreed.

"What do you think the little people were planning to do?" Willy asked.

But before Zack could answer, Willy found out for himself. The answer was hidden beneath Town Hall. As Willy lifted the building to pack it into a box, he drew in his breath.

"Look at this," he said to Zack.

"Whoa," Zack cried. "Some stash!"

The people of Tiny Town had been building an arsenal. Dozens of weapons had been made from objects they'd gathered from Willy's house. Paper clips and rubber bands had been turned into bows, and toothpicks into arrows. Margaret's fancy hair combs had been broken apart and the teeth transformed into swords. Peppercorns had been loaded into plastic rifles, and gum balls lay next to the cannon.

Most disturbing of all was the map that Willy found. Every room in the Tylers' house had been sketched on a small piece of paper.

"It looks like they were planning to take over the house!" Willy said when he saw it.

"With those dinky little weapons?" Zack scoffed. "Not likely!" He glanced at the map. "Where's your room on this thing?"

They scanned the map until they located Willy's room, right where it was supposed to be—upstairs, down the hall from Margaret's room.

Willy's heart stopped when he saw what was marked in the center of his room—a teeny, tiny bull's-eye.

Zack saw it too.

"Good thing we're packing up Tiny Town," Zack said in a low voice.

Willy nodded. He felt much safer now that all the little people were inside boxes tied up with string.

Yet an uneasy feeling kept gnawing away at him. At first, Willy couldn't quite put his finger on what it was that was bothering him. Then it came to him.

Hurley the Hobo was missing.

CHAPTER 20

Willy and Zack piled up the boxes in the corner of the basement.

"Willy!" Margaret screeched down the basement steps. "Mommy says get up here, right away!"

"Now what?" Willy groaned. "We can't be in any more trouble. Not when all the little people are packed up in boxes."

Willy's mom was waiting for them in the foyer. Margaret stood beside her in her butterfly costume.

"Come on, Mommy," Margaret whined as she tugged at her mother's arm. "We're going to be late for my recital."

Willy had to fight the urge to laugh at how stupid Margaret looked. But he didn't want to do anything that would make his mother even more angry than she already was.

"I'm taking Margaret to her dance recital," Mrs. Tyler informed them. "And I have half a mind to bring the two of you with me."

"Mom, no," Willy pleaded. "Don't do that!" Going to Margaret's dance recital was a fate worse than death.

"With the way you two have been behaving, I'm afraid to leave you alone," she went on.

Margaret snickered. "Your Tiny Town people might mess up the house again."

Mrs. Tyler hesitated. "Maybe I should just call a baby-sitter to stay with you all day until we get back."

"Moooooom!" Willy couldn't believe his mother would even suggest such a thing. "Zack and I are way too old for a baby-sitter!"

"Really, Mrs. Tyler," Zack chimed in. "Nothing bad is going to happen while you're gone. We're sure of it. All the little people are tied up in boxes—"

Willy elbowed Zack hard.

"I mean, we're not even going to talk about those little people again," Zack said quickly. "Like you said."

Finally Mrs. Tyler gave in. She turned to Willy. "If I come home and find one thing out of place," she threatened, "you can forget about going to Zack's house for two weeks. Do you understand me?"

Willy nodded.

"Margaret and I won't be home until close to dinnertime," she told them. "If your father gets home before I do, tell him that we'll all go out for pizza when I get back."

"Okay, Mom," Willy said.

"I meant what I said, Willy," Mrs. Tyler added as she and Margaret headed out the door.

Willy closed the door behind them.

"Oh, man," Zack sighed. "That was close."

"Tell me about it," Willy agreed.

Willy and Zack headed for the family room to crash in front of the TV. Thanks to Tiny Town, neither of them had slept very much over the past few days.

Willy plopped down on the couch. He was still worried about where Hurley the Hobo was hiding, but he forced himself to stop thinking about it.

What can one little plastic hobo do to us? he asked himself. *Nothing!*

Zack grabbed a pillow for his head as he stretched out on the floor. "What's on?"

"I don't know." Willy flicked through the channels.

Willy channel-surfed until Zack started to snore. Zack could fall asleep faster than anybody when he was really tired.

Willy was really tired too. So tired that for the first time, Zack's snores didn't keep him awake. Within a couple of minutes, Willy was sound asleep.

"Pull the ropes tighter!" a strange little voice whispered through Willy's dreams.

Willy felt something tickling his toe. He tried to rub it with his other foot, but his leg was so heavy. . . .

The tickling sensation moved across his foot and up his leg. He tried to open his eyes to see what it was. But he was in such a deep sleep, he couldn't seem to pull himself out of it.

Within seconds, every inch of Willy's skin felt as if it had come alive. Tiny little feet were creeping all over his body! Lots of them—on his legs, his arms, his stomach, his chest.

Willy tried to lift his hand, but it seemed to be pinned to the couch.

"Pull!" a voice commanded.

Suddenly Willy felt himself falling . . . and falling . . . and falling.

His heart started to pound furiously, the way it always did when he dreamed that he was falling. He hated the falling dream. He was always afraid that if he ever landed, something really terrible would happen to him. That's what everybody said about the falling dream—you couldn't land, or you might never wake up!

But Willy did land. Hard. And when he opened his eyes, he wasn't at all relieved to be awake.

Because something really was happening to him.

CHAPTER 21

Every part of Willy's body was bound and tied with the twine that he and Zack had used on the boxes of Tiny Town people.

But the Tiny Town people weren't in the boxes anymore. They were gathered around Willy. And they were definitely alive. They were laughing and shouting and walking all over him.

It wasn't just the Tiny Town people either. There were dozens of other toys. Toys that Willy hadn't played with in years, toys that his mom had stored away. There were Mutators and Aliens. Dinosaurs and Boogey Beasts. And more battle figures than all of the United States Armed Forces put together.

Every toy in the house was alive!

"Nooooooooooooo!" Willy screamed as he tried to struggle

free. But every time he tried to move, the little people pulled the twine even harder. It was wrapped around his limbs so tightly, he could feel it cutting into his flesh.

Willy really had fallen from the couch. But he'd landed on something that felt hard and scratchy. Whatever it was, it had wheels. Because every time the little people tugged on the ropes, Willy rolled forward. From the way he was balanced on the thing, it felt like a skateboard.

"So how does it feel to be toyed with, little man?" A voice sent chills up Willy's spine.

Willy wanted to scream. But fear strangled his throat as he watched Hurley the Hobo walk right up his chest.

"I told you to leave Tiny Town alone!" Hurley's haunting green eyes glimmered with malice. "But you just didn't want to listen to me, did you?"

"Answer him!" one of little knights demanded as he poked at Willy's throat with a tiny little sword.

"I'm sorry." Willy was so frightened, he could barely choke out the words. "We'll put Tiny Town back just the way you want it!"

Hurley started to laugh—the deepest, meanest laugh Willy had ever heard.

"It's too late for that," Hurley said. "We're done playing with you now. Take him away!" he told the little people.

"Zack!" Willy shouted as the skateboard lurched forward. But he didn't see Zack anywhere.

"Don't bother calling your friend," Hurley mocked as the little people continued to pull Willy through the family room. "He's already been defeated."

"Where is he?" Willy demanded.

"You'll find out soon enough," Hurley answered, laughing in Willy's face.

"Now *you're* going to pay for *your* crimes," one of the Weevils taunted as it wobbled up Willy's chest.

"Yeah," another little voice from the crowd cackled. "You're going to pay!"

Willy watched helplessly as the little people pulled him into the foyer. *Where are they taking me?* Willie wondered desperately.

The skateboard started to roll faster and faster toward the basement door.

Willy was sure the little people were going to send him toppling down the basement steps. Terror surged through him. There was no way in the world he'd ever survive that kind of fall.

"Open the prison door!" Hurley commanded.

Willy closed his eyes.

"Push him in with the other prisoner!" Hurley's voice bellowed.

Willy realized that he wasn't being pushed down the basement stairs, but into the hall closet.

Inside, Willy immediately saw Zack. He was tied and bound, just like Willy. Only there was a rubber ball crammed into his mouth as a gag.

"Zack!" Willy exclaimed. "You're alive!"

"Shut up!" Hurley ordered as the little knight held the sword to Willy's throat again. "From now on, you speak only when spoken to."

Willy had no choice but to obey as the little people dumped his body into the closet with Zack.

Hurley climbed onto a tiny horse.

"You may be alive for now," he threatened. "But I promise you, you're going to regret it!"

Willy watched in horror as the door to their prison slammed shut.

CHAPTER 22

"Let me out of here!" Willy screamed, kicking at the closet door.

He knew it was useless. But he couldn't think of anything else to do. Besides, somehow it made him feel better to kick and scream.

Zack was trying to scream too. But with the gag in his mouth, he could only grunt.

Suddenly Willy stopped screaming and kicking at the door. He didn't want the little people to come back and stuff a gag in his mouth too. The two boys needed a plan. And they needed one soon.

"Zack," Willy whispered.

But Zack didn't seem to hear him. He was still too busy trying to scream.

"Zack," Willy said a little louder.

Zack grunted.

"You've got to calm down," Willy told him. "We've got to think of a way to get out of here."

Zack seemed to be trying to tell Willy something, but with the rubber ball stuck in his mouth, Willy couldn't understand a word his friend was saying.

"Zack, listen to me," Willy ordered. Zack became quiet. "We've got to get back-to-back. That way we can try to untie each other. Okay?"

Zack grunted again. He understood.

This isn't going to be easy, Willy thought. For one thing, it was pitch black inside the closet. And there wasn't a lot of room for them to move around. Besides that, both boys had their hands tied behind their backs. Their ankles were tied together as well.

Willy and Zack shifted around in the cramped space like a couple of worms, crawling all over each other, trying to get into a sitting position. It took forever, but finally they succeeded.

"Let me try to untie you first," Willy whispered.

Slowly Willy untied the dozens of little knots in the twine. At last Willy managed to get Zack's hands free.

The first thing Zack did was pull the ball out of his mouth and start talking.

"Do you know how long I've been locked in this closet?" Zack complained. "I can't believe that you just lay there on the couch, sound asleep, while those little people tied me up and dragged me away. I was screaming and screaming for you to help me, but you didn't budge. Then they stuffed this ball in my mouth!"

Suddenly Willy wished he could stick the ball back in Zack's mouth.

"Shut up!" Willy hissed, trying to keep his voice low so that the little people wouldn't hear him. "Now untie me."

Zack shut up and went to work.

"So what do we do now?" Zack whispered once he'd untied Willy.

"We have to go out there," Willy whispered back.

"What if they're right outside that door waiting for us?" Zack asked nervously.

Willy was worried about that too. He pressed his ear against the door to see if he could hear them moving around. But all he heard was silence.

"I'm going to open the door just a crack and peek out," he told Zack.

Willy got on his knees and slid his hand up the door, feeling for the doorknob. He wrapped his hand around it and began to turn it very, very slowly. If there were any little people out there, he hoped they wouldn't notice the knob turning.

The door opened just a crack.

For a second, Willy was blinded by the light. He blinked hard a couple of times, then peeked out through the crack. There were no little people in sight.

Willy pushed the door open a little wider. Still nothing.

"Looks like the coast is clear," he whispered.

Together the two boys started to step out of the closet.

Suddenly, there was a loud, horrible shriek from above.

Willy looked up just in time. A hairy attacker was flying straight for his head!

CHAPTER 23

Willy hit the floor.

Margaret's Mookie Monster shrieked again as it plowed into Willy's back, knocking the wind out of him. Then it shot straight up to the ceiling again.

"Look out!" Zack screamed.

Willy stayed down, covering his head with his arms. The Mookie Monster hit him again. Hard. Again he bounced off Willy's back and flew up to the ceiling.

"He's coming again!" Zack shouted. He was pressed up against the wall, watching.

But before the monster touched down, Willy managed to scramble to his feet and get to the wall next to Zack.

This time the monster didn't bounce up to the ceiling. He hit the opposite wall instead, crashing into a family picture. Willy held his breath, waiting for the picture to fall and shatter on the floor.

The picture swung back and forth on its hook, but it stayed on the wall.

Before Willy could exhale, the monster shot straight across the foyer, knocking over a vase full of flowers. The vase crashed to the floor, exploding into a million pieces.

"We've got to stop him!" Willy screamed over the monster's shrieking.

"How?" Zack asked as the monster whizzed past them again.

The monster was bouncing around the room so fast, he was almost a blur. Willy tried to catch him, but his reflexes were too slow. The monster kept crisscrossing the room before Willy could even grab for him.

Finally Willy noticed that every time the monster hit the wall on their side of the room, he got closer and closer to the open closet.

Willy got behind the door, then waited and watched.

Bounce. Crash! Bounce. Crash! Bounce . . .

The monster went flying into the closet. Willy slammed the door shut fast. He heard the monster crash against the other side.

Willy leaned on the door with all of his weight, as the monster continued to crash against it.

"He's going to break down the door," Zack said, throwing his weight against it too.

"We can't let him get out," Willy said.

But they couldn't just stand there holding the door either. Not with the little people running loose in the house.

"Do you think you can hold it by yourself for a minute?" Willy asked Zack.

"Why?" Zack asked nervously. "Where are you going?"

"Into the kitchen to get a chair," Willy told him. "We can jam it under the doorknob to keep the door shut."

"Okay," Zack agreed reluctantly. "But hurry up."

Willy let go of the door. But he stayed for a second to make sure that Zack really could hold it by himself. Then he took off, running.

Willy was moving so fast, he didn't see the trip wire that the little people had pulled across the kitchen doorway.

Until it caught his ankle.

"Umpf!" Willy groaned as he went sailing face first across the kitchen floor. He didn't stop sliding until he crashed into the back door.

From the countertop came a terrible sound.

Slowly Willy lifted his head, afraid of what he'd see.

Sure enough, there stood Hurley, cackling as Willy lay sprawled on the floor.

CHAPTER 24

"Forces of Tiny Town, unite!" Hurley bellowed.

The second Hurley gave the order, every cabinet in the kitchen flew open at once. Willy watched in horror as Hurley's army started to pour out.

There were cowboys with rifles. Indians with spears. And dozens of archers carrying paper-clip bows loaded with sharp toothpick arrows.

From under the sink, the Aliens slimed into view. And from inside the sink, the Boogey Beasts climbed and clawed their way out of the garbage disposal.

Willy tried to get up. But he was so terrified, his feet slid out from under him.

Hurley's forces were closing in on Willy from every side.

From the dining room, the Civil War soldiers charged,

dragging cannons and catapults. From behind the refrigerator came the knights on their steeds, waving their swords and jousting spears. Above Willy, the Mutators swooped down from the air vents, transforming themselves into robots with rocket arms as they hit the floor.

"Archers, take aim!" Hurley commanded.

Willy scrambled to get up. But as he did, Hurley shouted, "Fire!"

Hundreds of toothpick arrows soared through the air.

Willy put up his hand to cover his eyes as the sharp points pricked him everywhere. They cut right through his flesh and stuck in his skin.

"Zack!" Willy cried out. "Help!"

But Zack didn't hear him. He was too busy screaming for Willy.

"Willy!" Zack came running into the kitchen. "The Mookie Monster got out! And he's trying to bite my butt!"

Zack stopped dead in his tracks. The Mookie Monster flew right past him, bouncing off the walls until he landed near Hurley.

"What the heck is going on?" Zack cried as he tried to shield himself from the flying toothpicks.

"War!" Hurley shouted maliciously. "War!"

The archers started moving in for the kill.

"Oooouch!" Zack screamed as one of the toothpicks hit him in the nose. "These things really hurt!"

"I know," Willy shot back as he pulled a tiny arrow from his neck.

"Cut it out!" Zack shouted, kicking at the group of archers who started to circle his feet. Six of them went sailing across the room. But the ones who didn't continued firing.

Willy reached down to grab an archer who was aiming right for his eyes. "Give me that thing!" Willy screamed as he tried to pull the bow from the archer's hand. But the archer kept struggling. Willy couldn't believe how strong he was.

Willy pulled as hard as he could. The archer's arm came off, but he didn't seem to notice. He kept kicking and squiggling to get free.

"Gross!" Willy cried as he threw the little guy across the room.

"We can't even hurt them!" Zack cried.

"Riflemen," Hurley shouted. "Prepare to fire!"

Every little man with a rifle started to move forward. Willy and Zack started to back up.

Just then, one of the Weevils wobbled across the floor and tugged on Willy's sock.

"Now you're really going to pay!"

"Shut up, you creepy little Weevil!" Willy shouted as he kicked the Weevil right in the face.

The Weevil wobbled, but he didn't fall down. Then he bit Willy's ankle. Hard.

"Fire!" Hurley ordered.

Within seconds, hundreds of peppercorns tore through the air, pelting Willy and Zack like BBs. They hit so hard, Willy could actually see welts starting to erupt on his skin.

Willy and Zack tried to fight back, but it was useless. The more they kicked and swatted at the little people, the more the figures kept on coming.

Hurley and his army were forcing Willy and Zack to retreat, backing them all the way out into the foyer.

"Bring in the cannons!" Hurley shouted.

The riflemen parted lines as dozens of other men pulled the cannons and catapults onto the tiled floor.

"Fire!" Hurley commanded.

A rainbow of gum balls exploded from the cannons with terrifying force. Willy ducked, afraid they would tear right through him like real bullets. As they hit the walls, the gum balls left pink, red, purple, and blue stains.

"Run!" Willy shouted at Zack. But there was nowhere to go. Hurley and his army had backed Willy and Zack all the way up to the front door.

"Cease fire!" Hurley ordered.

Suddenly, the little men lowered their weapons. The cannons stopped booming.

Willy didn't move. Neither did Zack. They just watched in horror as one of the Mutator rockets swooped up Hurley, then flew him right into their faces.

"You have one choice," Hurley said as he hovered in front of Willy's nose. "Get out or be destroyed!"

CHAPTER 25

Willy's mind was racing even faster than his heart. He knew that if he and Zack left the house, they'd never get back in. The little people would take it over for good. But if they stayed, they'd never make it *out* of the house again. At least, not alive. Hurley and his army had made that very clear.

"What's it going to be?" Hurley hovered above Willy like a giant cloud of doom.

"Come on, Willy," Zack whispered. "Let's go!"

Willy's eyes darted about the foyer. He wasn't ready to give up. Desperately he tried to figure out a way to get past Hurley and his army.

Less than six feet in front of him were the steps leading upstairs. If he and Zack could just get to the steps, they might be able to make it to his room. Then maybe they could figure out a war plan of their own.

"I'm waiting," Hurley stated coldly. "What are you going to do?" The Mutator's rocket engine revved, sending black puffs of smoke billowing through the foyer.

"Come on, Zack!" Willy shouted. "Run for the stairs!"

Willy and Zack took off, ducking under Hurley and the rocket. They tore through the group of cavalry men by the stairs, knocking dozens of them off their tiny horses.

"We have to get to my room!" Willy screamed as they reached the first step.

Immediately Hurley called in his reserves.

"Airborne unit!" Hurley beckoned. "Engage!"

Suddenly the sound of choppers echoed through the foyer as dozens of military helicopters took flight.

"Open fire!" Hurley shouted.

Willy couldn't believe it. The miniature choppers started firing machine guns. Machine guns loaded with shiny red beads from Margaret's jewelry-making kit!

Willy could feel the beads stinging his skin as they pelted him. Hard. And fast.

"We're never going to make it!" Zack cried out.

"We have to!" Willy hollered.

Zack reached up to swat one of the choppers circling his head. He hit it so hard it crashed down to the foyer floor.

"Way to go!" Willy exclaimed as he watched the chopper smash into pieces.

Willy reached up to do the same thing. With one hard swing, he sent three more choppers swirling into fatal tailspins.

"Let's go!" Willy shouted as they reached the top of the stairs. Ahead of them, the coast looked clear. But behind them, Willy heard the sound of more choppers revving their engines.

Willy and Zack tore down the hall. When they reached Willy's parents' room, Willy froze. Inside the room, Suzie Sparkle and her friends were having a party, playing dress-up with Willy's mom's clothing. Perfume bottles were knocked over on top of the dresser, and perfume was spilling onto the carpet. The mirror and bedspread were covered with red lipstick. And Mrs. Tyler's diamond bracelet was wrapped around Suzie Sparkle's neck like a giant necklace.

"Come on, Willy!" Zack grabbed his arm. "Don't worry about that stupid doll. We have to keep going!"

But before Willy could move, he heard a screech from behind him. He spun around. Coming at him was a flying dragon, its fangs bared.

"Watch out!" Zack screamed as the dragon roared, aiming its fiery breath at Willy's face.

"Oooooooch!" Willy cried as the flame licked his nose.

"Let's get out of here!" Zack screamed.

But just as Willy and Zack took off for Willy's room, dozens of fire-breathing flying dragons swooped down for the kill.

Willy and Zack were about to fry.

CHAPTER 26

Willy and Zack made it into Willy's room without a second to spare. As Willy slammed the door behind them, he could hear the dragons crashing into it.

"Lock it!" Zack screamed.

He didn't have to tell Willy that. The door was locked even before Zack finished speaking.

Willy quickly looked around the room, just to make sure that he and Zack were really alone. They had to figure out their next move.

"I'm shot up pretty bad," Willy said grimly as he inspected his battle wounds. "And that dragon burned my nose."

Zack was inspecting his wounds too. "I guess we shouldn't have made fun of their little weapons," he said, rubbing the welts on his arms. "Those little weapons did some big damage."

Almost every part of Willy's body hurt. But he was too angry to give up. "They may have done some damage," he said. "But they're not going to win this war."

"How do you figure that?" Zack asked, sounding pretty defeated. "*They've* taken over the whole house, while *we're* hiding out in the bedroom."

"We're not hiding out," Willy insisted. "We're regrouping." Zack rolled his eyes.

"I mean it, Zack," Willy told him. "We can't let them win."

"They already have," Zack said. "We've kicked them. We've stepped on them. We've even ripped their arms off. Nothing stops them."

"Then we have to catch them," Willy said, "and lock them up somehow, so they can't escape."

"How?" Zack wanted to know. "We can't get near them. Not without getting stabbed, shot at, or burned."

"We need to protect ourselves," Willy said, heading for his closet. He started tossing all his sports equipment out of the closet. There were knee pads, elbow pads, helmets, even goggles.

"Now all we need is a way to capture them," Zack said.

The two of them sat there, quietly thinking as they started putting on their protective gear.

Willy heard something moving around on the other side of the room. It was a metallic sound. And it was coming from the air vent.

Suddenly the vent cover exploded off the wall. Dozens of knights in shining armor started dropping out onto the floor. They rushed Willy and Zack with their swords drawn.

Zack was sitting closer to the vent. He tried to get away as the knights reached him. Desperately he pushed himself backward across the carpet.

The first knight drove his lance into Zack's ankle. Zack reached out to swat him away. But the instant his hand made contact with the knight, there was a huge spark. *"Ooooouch!"* Zack cried out in pain.

Willy's eyes stayed fixed on the knight as electricity shot through the tiny figure.

CHAPTER 27

Willy couldn't believe his eyes.

No one moved as the little knight stood in the center of the room, crackling with electricity. Finally, the sparks died and the knight fell over.

"You zapped him to death!" Willy cried.

The rest of the knights continued marching toward Zack and Willy.

"See if you can get another one," Willy yelled as little swords were thrust at him from all directions.

Zack swatted at another knight. But nothing happened.

"You've got to juice yourself up first," Willy reminded him.

Zack quickly rubbed his feet on the carpet to build up a good supply of static electricity. Then he struck out again.

"It works!" Willy's fist punched the air as the second knight fizzled out. "Keep it up," he told Zack. "Get them all!"

"I don't know if I can," Zack said. "This hurts me too, you know. It's much worse than zapping a regular person."

"I know," Willy said. "But it's our only hope, Zack. You've got to do it."

Zack kept at it, zapping knight after knight.

Willy rubbed his feet furiously on the carpet, trying to build up enough static electricity so that he could help Zack. But it didn't work for him. For some reason, only Zack could do it.

Willy couldn't help Zack shock the little knights, but he *could* prevent them from getting away. Willy went over to the air vent and blocked it so that none of the knights could escape. He didn't want word to get back to Hurley that he and Zack had finally found a way to stop his army.

"Way to go!" Willy cheered as Zack zapped the last knight. "Now let's go get the rest of them."

"Are you crazy?" Zack said. "There are hundreds of them out there! I can't zap them all."

"Sure you can," Willy encouraged him. "It's the only way, Zack . . ."

There was silence. They both knew what would happen if Zack didn't keep it up.

Willy let Zack rest for a couple of minutes while he came up with a plan.

"Okay," Willy said at last. "Here's what I think. Hurley's army is right outside that door, ready to attack. So what I'm going to do is open the door just long enough for a few of them to get through. Then, once you've zapped them, I'll let a few more in. We'll get as many as we can like that. Maybe even all of them."

Willy headed over to the door and unlocked it. "Ready?" he asked Zack.

Zack nodded.

"Here goes." Willy opened the door, ready to slam it shut as soon as the little people started pouring in.

But the little people didn't come.

Willy stuck his head out into the hallway to look around. The hallway was deserted.

"Where are they?" Zack asked Willy.

Willy held a finger to his lips. He was sure they were out there someplace.

"What's going on?" Zack came to the door.

"Shh," Willy told him. He'd heard something and was trying to figure out what it was.

When Zack stopped talking, Willy heard the sound again. It was the sound of water running, and it was coming from the bathroom.

Willy stepped out into the hallway to listen more carefully. He began to hear voices coming from the bathroom, then high-pitched giggles.

"Do you hear that?" he whispered to Zack.

Zack nodded. "It sounds like someone's having a party in there."

Willy started walking cautiously toward the bathroom. Zack followed him. The sounds grew louder as they approached.

The door was wide open.

Willy peeked through the doorway to see what was going on. A party *was* happening in there. A pool party!

Suzie Sparkle and all her friends were dressed in bathing suits, sitting on the bathtub ledge.

Willy motioned for Zack to have a look too.

"Last one in the pool is a rotten egg," Suzie Sparkle shouted.

All the dolls hit the water at once. Huge sparks flew out of the tub as the water bubbled and churned.

Zack looked at Willy. "What's going on?" he whispered.

Willy thought he knew, but he didn't want to say anything until he was sure.

Willy opened the door wider to get a better look. What he saw was exactly what he'd been hoping to see.

Suzie Sparkle and her friends were floating on top of the water, totally lifeless.

"The water zapped them!" Zack exclaimed. "They didn't know it would electrocute them."

"Right!" Willy said. "This is so great," he added as a wicked grin spread across his face. "If they didn't know, then maybe Hurley doesn't know either."

Zack grinned back. "You know what we need?" he said. "A couple of water pistols."

"I've got something better than water pistols," Willy told him. "I've got Super Dooper Power Blasters."

"Cool!" Zack's whole face lit up. "The war is over now."

"Not quite," Willy told him. There was bad news too.

"What are you talking about?" Zack asked.

"The Power Blasters aren't in my room," Willy told him. "Before we can beat Hurley's army, we've got to make it to the garage."

CHAPTER 28

"No matter what happens," Willy told Zack as they started racing down the hall like two commandos, "we can't stop!"

"Gotcha," Zack agreed. "I'm right behind you!"

Only Zack wasn't the only thing right behind Willy. Suddenly something slimy and wet hit the back of Willy's neck.

Whatever it was, it was squiggling and squirming like a giant blob of jelly. Its long, slimy tentacles started to wrap themselves around Willy's throat.

"Zack!" Willy screamed. "What's this gross thing on me?"

"Aaaaaagh!" Zack cried out. "Something's sliming me!"

Willy spun around fast to see dozens of Alien creatures slithering across the ceiling. They were creeping up from behind and dropping down to attack.

"Say hello to the Alien Nation," Hurley laughed as he whizzed by them on his Mutator rocket.

"Do something!" Zack screamed. He wrestled with the slimy green Alien attached to the side of his face. "He's trying to suck my face off!"

There was no way for Willy to help Zack. Not while he had an Alien of his own stuck on his neck, trying to strangle the life out of him.

Willy grabbed the tentacles around his throat, pulling so hard that he managed to rip them right off the Alien. Then he grabbed the blob on the back of his neck and threw it at the ceiling, knocking a bunch of the Aliens to the floor a few feet back down the hall.

"Help!" Zack cried out in pain.

Willy tried to pull the green ball of slime off the side of Zack's face. But it wouldn't let go.

"You've got to zap him!" Willy hollered at Zack.

"I tried!" Zack cried out. "I must be out of juice!"

Willy knew there was no way to get Zack back to the bathroom, where he could stick his face under some water. The rest of the Aliens were closing in way too fast. And they were way too fierce.

So Willy did the only thing he could think of. He mustered up all the spit in his mouth and sent it hurtling toward Zack's face.

As the spit made contact, the Alien let out a hissing sound. Smoke rose from its quivering body as it dropped onto the floor.

"Oh, man." Zack cringed as he wiped the rest of Willy's

spit from his cheek. "You spit ᴀᴛ me!"

"Lucky for you," Willy retorted. "Otherwise that Alien would have sucked your whole face off!"

Zack couldn't argue with that, no matter how grossed out he was.

Quickly Willy grabbed him by the arm and fled for the stairs. The Aliens were right behind them. They covered the hallway like living, breathing, oozing wallpaper.

Up ahead, Willy could see Hurley's army marching up the steps.

"Now what?" Zack said.

"Just plow right through them!" Willy told him.

Willy and Zack had no choice. Luckily, the protective sports gear they had put on earlier shielded them from the bullets and arrows that flew at them from all sides. They raced down the steps like a tornado, sending dozens of Hurley's little soldiers spinning through the air.

The second they hit the foyer, the Weevils wobbled into view.

"You can run," one of the Weevils hollered, "but you're still going to die!"

Willy looked at Zack. His friend was thinking the exact same thing.

"I don't think so," Willy taunted as he and Zack leaned over the entire Weevil family. Then, at the same time, Willy and Zack sent two giant globs of spit hurtling down at the Weevils.

"Yes!" Willy and Zack high-fived each other as the Weevils wobbled and finally fell down.

But there was no time to celebrate. They had to get to the garage for the water guns.

Once they made it through the foyer, getting to the garage was a cinch. The coast was clear. Willy was sure it was because all of Hurley's forces had gathered upstairs.

As it turned out, Willy was wrong.

CHAPTER
29

Willy and Zack grabbed the Super Dooper Power Blasters, then rushed back into the kitchen to fill them up.

"Prepare to die!" Hurley bellowed as he soared into the kitchen, followed by an entire army of Mutators.

Willy's eyes nearly popped out as he took in the sight of the biggest and baddest unit in Hurley's army.

All at once, the Mutator rockets fired laser beams that tore through the kitchen like radioactive lightning bolts. The air attack was immediately followed by a ground attack. Mutated robots rolled into the kitchen, blasting endless streams of rocket fire from their mutator arms.

As the neon beams of destruction hit Willy and Zack, they burned holes through their armor. Whatever the Mutators were firing was real. And as deadly as Hurley had promised.

"Hurry up!" Willy yelled. Zack was frantically trying to fill up one of the guns. "They're shooting real lasers!"

"I'm going as fast as I can!" Zack cried as a burning blue beam fried a hole through the top of his football helmet.

Willy knew there was no way Zack could do it. There was no way to fill the Power Blasters fast enough to wipe out the Mutators before the Mutators wiped them out.

"Say your final good-byes!" Hurley laughed as the Mutator rockets swooped into a *V* formation, ready to open fire at close range.

"Noooooo!" Willy lunged for the spray hose attached to the sink. He turned the faucet on full blast and squeezed the nozzle on the hose as hard as he could. Water sprayed through the air with such force, the Mutators started dropping like flies.

Willy sprayed the ceiling and the walls and the floors. He fired and fired until all the Mutators crackled with defeat. By the time Willy stopped shooting, there wasn't a live Mutator in sight. The kitchen floor was one giant slip-and-slide.

"Way to go!" Zack exclaimed as Willy slid across the linoleum.

But Willy was looking for Hurley.

Only Hurley was nowhere to be seen.

"He got away!" Willy cried as he searched through the Mutator casualties. "I can't believe it!"

"Don't worry about it," Zack insisted as he started to fill up the guns again. "We'll get him!"

Willy was sure Zack was right. Once they armed themselves with the Power Blasters, all they had to do was storm through the house and fire away.

In no time at all, Willy and Zack had wiped out all the little people left in the house. They reclaimed the stairs and the hallway, bringing down the Aliens with the Super Dooper Power Blasters. They cleared out room after room, making sure that nothing was left in their path. They even fired streams of water into the air vents, just in case.

Now all they had to do was find Hurley.

"He's got to be in this house somewhere," Willy insisted as he and Zack headed down to the basement. "Are you sure you searched down here?"

"Six times," Zack told him. "There was nobody down here. Maybe he fell down a vent. I'm telling you, there's no way Hurley made it out of this war alive."

Zack was wrong.

Willy knew it the minute he entered the basement. His heart started to pound.

Sitting on the table that used to hold Tiny Town was Hurley the Hobo's little bench. The tiny bundle was gone. But pinned to the back of the bench was another tiny note.

"Uh-oh," Zack gasped when he saw it. "He can't be planning another war," he said. "Everybody's dead!"

Willy was sure that was true. He and Zack had already collected six or seven garbage bags full of toys—every toy that Willy had ever owned, along with Margaret's Mookie Monster and the rest of her goofy dolls. So unless Hurley had a bunch of tiny toy friends on the outside, there was no way he could wage another war.

Nervously, Willy pulled the note off the bench. He headed over to his father's tool closet for the magnifying glass.

"What does it say?" Zack asked anxiously.

Willy read the note again.

"Come on, Willy! Tell me what it says!" Zack demanded.

Willy looked up and smiled. For the first time, he actually got a kick out of a note from Hurley.

"'Don't bother looking for me,'" Willy read aloud. "'You won't find me. I'm moving out. And I'm moving on. Hurley.'"

"Moving on to where?" Zack asked.

"Who cares?" Willy laughed. "He's gone!"

"What a weenie!" Zack laughed too. "He ran away because he knew we were going to kick his butt!"

"He's going to get his butt kicked anyway," Willy said. "There's no way he can make it out in the real world. He's only a couple of inches tall."

"Yeah," Zack added. "And the first time it rains, he's dead."

The thrill of victory finally started to sink in. This time Willy and Zack really did do a victory dance.

No one would believe it, but they had defeated an entire army of toys armed with powerful weapons.

"High five!" Willy exclaimed as Zack slapped his hand.

The terror of Tiny Town was finally gone for good!

CHAPTER 30

The thrill of victory soon gave way to the agony of defeat. The war with Tiny Town wasn't the only battle Willy and Zack had to fight. There was another war, with much bigger people. Namely, Willy's parents. And it went on for days.

When Willy's mom got home, most of the house was still in a shambles. Willy knew there was no point in trying to convince his parents that the house was a mess because he and Zack had been fighting for their lives against the little people, even though they both had the battle wounds to prove it.

Blaming Hurley and his armies would only have made things worse. Willy and Zack had no choice but to plead insanity and take the rap.

The yelling went on and on. No matter what Willy or

Zack said or did, Willy's parents swore they weren't going to let Willy go home with Zack.

It lasted right up until the night before they were supposed to leave.

Finally Mr. Tyler caved in to the boys' pleas. He convinced Mrs. Tyler to grant them a pardon. Willy was sure the only reason his mom gave in was because she wanted a two-week vacation from him.

"Are you sure you have everything you need?" Mrs. Tyler asked as Willy and Zack climbed up the platform for the train.

"Yeah, Mom," Willy answered as he struggled with his suitcases. Willy had more than he needed. He had packed nearly his whole room.

"You promise you'll behave for Mrs. Miller." It wasn't a question. It was an order.

"Don't worry, Mom," Willy told her. "I'll be on my best behavior. I promise."

"If I hear one bad report, Willy," she threatened, "you will never visit Zack again. Understand?"

"Yeah, Mom," Willy answered. "I understand."

It was pouring rain. Margaret was whining up a storm about getting wet, even though they were standing on a covered platform.

"Come on, Mommy," Margaret moaned. "Just kiss them good-bye and let's go home!"

For the first time, Willy was grateful that Margaret was moaning. He wanted to get on the train already so that he and Zack could finally have some fun.

"In a minute, Margaret," his mother scolded. Then she turned her attention back to the boys. "Do you have your train tickets?"

"Yes," Willy answered, growing more impatient.

Thunder rumbled in the distance, and the rain started coming down harder.

"All right," his mother said with a sigh. "You two better get on the train. And Margaret and I had better get back to the car in case lightning starts." She kissed both boys. "Are you sure you'll be okay?"

"We'll be fine," Willy assured her again, picking up his bags.

"Be good," she called after them as they headed for the train.

"Bye, Margaret," Willy said, thrilled about getting away from her for two weeks.

"Yeah, bye, Margaret," Zack echoed. "Bye, Mrs. Tyler. Thanks for everything."

Margaret waved as she and Mrs. Tyler headed off the platform.

Willy and Zack boarded the train, happy to be on their own at last. This was the moment they'd been waiting for, and it felt great.

To make matters even better, they found an empty car.

"This is too cool," Willy exclaimed, settling into a seat next to the window.

"Yeah," Zack agreed, taking the seat facing Willy's. "I hope nobody else comes into this car."

It looked like Zack was going to get his wish. The train whistle blew. The engine started. The train was ready to leave the station, and the two boys still had the car to themselves.

Willy looked out the window. The storm was getting worse. He saw a flash of lightning and heard the thunder rumble louder. He was glad he and Zack were safely on the train.

The platform was deserted now. All the benches were empty.

All but one.

Willy's blood ran cold.

"Zack," Willy said, poking his friend. "Look at that bench near the ticket booth."

Zack looked out the window. "Yeah? What about it?"

"What's that thing sitting on it?" Willy asked nervously.

"I don't know." Zack squinted to see better. "It looks like a toy or something."

"It looks like Hurley," Willy said.

"No way," Zack replied with a laugh.

"Look closer," Willy told him.

But before Zack could look again, there was a blinding flash of lightning right outside the window. Thunder hit like a bomb, shaking the whole train.

Willy's heart skipped a beat. It skipped another beat when he looked out the window again at the bench where he thought he'd seen Hurley the Hobo.

Hurley was there all right. Only he wasn't a little toy hobo anymore. He was life-size.

He sat on the bench with his sack resting over his shoulder, looking directly at Willy. His piercing green eyes cut right through the storm and sent a chill up Willy's spine.

"Zack," Willy gasped. "Look!"

"I see," Zack answered, sounding as terrified as Willy felt.

Hurley waved to the boys as the train began to pull out of the station.

"Hurry up!" Willy cried, wishing he could will the train to move faster. He wanted to get as far away from Hurley the Hobo as he could.

But that wasn't going to happen.

As the train chugged slowly down the track, Hurley the Hobo got up from his bench and hopped aboard.

Willy and Zack screamed in horror as the conductor's voice came over the loudspeaker.

"Next and only stop, Tiny Town!"

Get ready for more . . .

*Here's a preview of the next spine-chilling book
from A. G. Cascone*

INVASION OF THE APPLEHEADS

For Robin and Andy Carter, a day of sight-seeing with their parents is about to turn into a nightmare when they arrive at the old Appleton Orchard.

As they entered the grounds, Robin felt something strange. Something that made her shiver. It was as if she'd passed through some kind of invisible wall, or like diving into a pool and breaking through the surface of the water. And it happened just as quickly.

Strangely, outside the gates, the trees were turning colors and losing their leaves, but inside the gates, the apple trees were in full bloom—green and loaded with fruit.

Robin turned around in her seat to look back at the gates.

Something else was wrong. But it took Robin a minute to figure out what it was.

Outside the gates, where the leaves on the trees were dying, it was a beautiful, sunny day. But inside the gates, where everything blossomed, it was dark and dreary.

Robin shivered again. "Creepy," she said, talking to herself.

"What's creepy?" her mother asked.

"The trees," Robin answered. "How come they've still got apples?"

"Maybe the apple season is longer out here in the country," her mother said.

"But look how dark it is in here," Robin pointed out.

Her father laughed. "Of course it's dark," he said. "We're in the shadow of all these trees."

Robin caught a glimpse of the sky above the trees. It was steely gray, with no sunshine at all.

But before Robin could point that out to her family, the words stuck in her throat as a hideous creature stepped out from between the apple trees that lined the drive. Its head was swollen, and the green, putrid skin that covered its face was rotting right off its skull. Bloodshot eyeballs hung from their sockets. And a blood-covered ax stuck out of its chest.

"Look!" Mrs. Carter laughed as another grotesque creature appeared ahead of them. "Everyone is dressed up for Halloween!"

Robin took a good look at the creature with the ax in its chest. If that was a costume, it was very, very good.

"This is excellent!" Andy said. "I definitely want to go on the haunted hayride."

"Didn't I tell you this would be fun?" Mrs. Carter said.

They pulled into the parking lot under a giant old shade tree where several other cars were already parked. But there were no other people in sight. Just the biggest, creepiest-looking scarecrow on a pole that Robin had ever seen.

Its head was the size of a basketball, and it was covered with a dirty white sheet that was tied around its neck with a thick, heavy rope dangling to the ground like a leash. Its face was painted onto the sheet.

The second her father parked the car, the creature started to move!

Robin let out a loud, startled cry.

So did her mother.

"It's all right," Robin's father assured them. "It's just

someone dressed up in a Halloween costume."

The giant creature climbed down from its pole and started clomping its way toward them, flailing its arms and moaning. It looked like Frankenstein's monster dressed up as a scarecrow.

No one made a move to get out of the car.

"If he's trying to scare us away, he's doing a pretty good job." Robin's mother chuckled nervously.

The scarecrow fell onto the hood of the car, moaning and groaning even louder than before.

"Let's get out of here!" Robin cried.

But it was too late.

Within seconds, the car was surrounded by cackling witches and blood-covered ghouls.

And Robin had the horrible feeling that they weren't just people in Halloween costumes. . . .

Collect them all!

About the Author

A. G. Cascone is the pseudonym of two authors. Between them, they have written six previous books, two horror movie screenplays, and several pop songs, including one top-ten hit.

If you want to find out more about DEADTIME STORIES or A. G. Cascone, look on the World Wide Web at:
        http://www.bookwire.com/titles/deadtime/

Also, we'd love to hear from you! You can write to
        A. G. Cascone
        c/o Troll
        100 Corporate Drive
        Mahwah, NJ 07430–1404

Or you can send e-mail directly to:
        agcascone@bookwire.com